ALSO BY ALYSON NOËL

FOR TEENS

THE SOUL SEEKERS SERIES

Fated
Echo
Mystic
Horizon

THE IMMORTALS SERIES

Evermore
Blue Moon
Shadowland
Dark Flame
Night Star
Everlasting

THE BEAUTIFUL IDOLS SERIES

Unrivaled
Blacklist
Infamous

●—●

Cruel Summer
Saving Zoë
Kiss & Blog
Fly Me to the Moon
Laguna Cove
Art Geeks and Prom Queens
Faking 19

●—●

FOR TWEENS

THE RILEY BLOOM SERIES

Radiance
Shimmer
Dreamland
Whisper

Five Days of Famous

THE BONE THIEF

ALYSON NOËL

DELACORTE PRESS

Text copyright © 2017 by Alyson Noël LLC
Jacket art and interior illustrations copyright © 2017 by Vincent Chong

randomhousekids.com

Educators and librarians, for a variety of teaching tools,
visit us at RHTeachersLibrarians.com

Library of Congress Cataloging-in-Publication Data is available upon request.

ISBN 978-0-553-53800-7 (trade) — ISBN 978-0-553-53802-1 (ebook)

The text of this book is set in 12-point Adobe Caslon.
Interior design by Ken Crossland

Printed in the United States of America
10 9 8 7 6 5 4 3 2 1
First Edition

For those who fear they're different.

And for those who think they're normal.

It's weird not to be weird.

—John Lennon

A BRIEF NOTE ABOUT QUIVER HOLLOWS

If you've never been to Quiver Hollows (and let's face it, most people haven't), then you've probably never been forced to ride your bike onto a perpetually frozen lake to avoid crashing into a fluffle of blue bunnies idly crossing the road.

It's also entirely possible that you've never watched a dog give birth to a litter of purple piglets.

And with that in mind, it's safe to assume you've also never seen a waterfall flow in a loop. (For the record, it looks like a water zipper—zooming straight from the bottom to the top and then back again.)

In fact, if you've never visited Quiver Hollows (and why would you, since you've probably never even heard of it until now?), then there's a very good chance you doubt these sorts of things can exist.

So later, when you read about a girl named Ming who can levitate high above the treetops, a boy named Ollie who can bend metal using only his mind, and another girl, Penelope, who can communicate through the images she creates in her head, you'll probably doubt they exist too.

By this point you may even suspect you're reading the words of a pathological liar. A person who is downright delusional, and who absolutely, positively cannot be trusted and is better avoided.

But that's only because you've never set foot in Quiver Hollows.

If you had, you'd be nodding in solidarity, secure in the knowledge that the world is indeed so much stranger than it seems.

ONE

PROFESSOR SNELLING'S SCHOOL FOR SPOON BENDING

Professor Snelling swipes a spoon from the top of my pile, pinches the base between his forefinger and thumb, and using only the powers of his mind, bends it first into a circle, then a heart, before finishing with a five-pointed star.

"See, Grimsly—see how easy and uncomplicated it is? And it all begins and ends here." He taps a long, twisted talon to his temple and nods encouragingly, and if I didn't know better, I'd think he was bragging. But the truth is, I've seen him make much more complicated shapes in a lot less time. As far as spoon benders go, Professor Snelling is considered the best in Quiver Hollows—almost as good as our town's founder, Yegor Quiver, which is really saying something.

With the tips of his curlicue mustache twitching and the flesh around his eyes crinkling like origami, Snelling looks at me and says, "Now let's see you try. But first—what's the secret to spoon-bending success?"

I clear my throat, straighten my shoulders, and in a clear, strong voice recite the words on the silver-framed sign hanging on the opposite wall.

TO ACHIEVE IT, YOU FIRST
HAVE TO SEE IT AND BELIEVE IT.
IMAGINATION IS KEY!

Just to be clear, it's not like I needed to read straight from the sign. The words are part of our daily drills. They're practically tattooed on my brain.

Still, on an important day like today—the day of the sixth-grade final spoon-bending exam—my confidence is running so low I can't afford to take any risks.

Despite the countless hours of careful instruction—despite all my classmates' having grasped the art from the very first day only to spend the rest of the semester improving their skills—I'm still no closer to performing the sort of mental magic required of spoon bending than I was on the very first day in this class. And as much as I'm hoping that today is the day when all those lessons will begin to make sense and I'll find myself twisting this heaping pile of spoons into unrecognizable silver bits, fact is I'll be lucky if I can manage just enough of a crook in one handle to walk out of this room with some slim shred of dignity intact.

Everyone in Quiver Hollows has a thing—at least one major peculiarity (and sometimes as many as two or three) that makes them really different, extremely odd, and unique.

Everyone except me, that is. The only odd thing about me is I'm as normal, average, and boring as a person can be.

Snelling grins in a way that sets his face into a riot of wrinkles that obscures everything but his nose, which remains splendidly long, triumphantly hooklike, and completely unaffected by the rest of his features. He plucks another spoon from the top of the pile and presents it with great flourish, and when he places it before me, I instantly break into a cold, clammy sweat. There's no more delaying. The moment has come.

"Grimsly," he says, his voice assuming a more serious, professorial tone. "You can do this, you'll see. Just remember what I taught you—all that's required is a dash of mind magic and the belief that you can."

I settle near the edge of my seat and frown. It's not that

I doubt what he says, but it's becoming increasingly obvious that what's true for Professor Snelling is not necessarily true for me.

I glance around the room. My focus moves from the oversized gilt-framed portrait of Yegor Quiver, his wise, all-seeing gaze aiming to inspire us from beyond the grave, to the large glass-fronted display case crammed with all manner of intricately contorted metal sculptures crafted by Professor Snelling's former students, to the glistening mobiles hanging overhead fashioned entirely of twisted gold and silver cutlery before turning hesitantly toward the single unyielding spoon lying before me.

"You know the rules," he says. "Exactly one minute for the lot."

Then, just when I'm sure he's decided to cut me some slack by giving me one less spoon to worry about, he plucks the star from the table and with a blink returns it to its original shape and places it on top of the heap.

Great. Sixty spoons in sixty seconds. Only a miracle can save me now.

I take a deep breath and look at the words of inspiration scrawled across the chalkboard:

FOCUS! CONCENTRATE! IMAGINE! BELIEVE!
THAT'S ALL THERE IS TO IT—YOU'LL SEE!

It sounds reasonable enough in theory, but after watching Snelling plow through his own pile of spoons before he was forced to delve into mine, molding them easily, as though they were made of rubber, it's time to face the unavoidable truth: I'm about to become the very first person in Quiver Hollows to ever fail the spoon-bending exam. Exactly the sort of distinction I'd prefer not to claim.

With a simple nod, Professor Snelling makes a quick jab at the pocket watch he pulls from his robe and the wall of clocks reset to zero. The countdown is on.

The second hand begins its descent, sending time marching forward with an audible *tick-tick-tick* as I close my eyes and go through the steps. First I picture a circle looming large in my head, and since my expectations are already low, it's not even a perfect circle. Its sides are uneven, with one popped out, the other pushed in—the sort of thing even the most challenged student should be able to replicate. Then I follow the short list of steps that for the last several months have been drilled into my brain.

I focus.

Concentrate.

And believe in that lopsided circle with all my heart.

And then . . .

Something extraordinary happens.

Something that seems almost too good to be true.

The spoon begins to curve in a place where it once used to be straight!

Since my eyes are closed in deep concentration, it's not like I can actually see it, but somehow I just know that stubborn slab of metal is finally, magically, yielding to my forces of will. And while it's only one spoon, I no longer doubt that the others will follow.

When the sixty seconds are up, the collection of clocks gets to buzzing so loudly the whole room seems to vibrate. I snap my eyes open and plant a wide grin on my face in anticipation of the celebration to come.

Until I catch Professor Snelling's look of despair. He stares unbelievingly at the single unremarkable spoon lying stupidly before me. My grin fades as I realize that whatever images I saw in my head, whatever sensations I felt in my heart, none of them managed to find their way out. The spoon is exactly the same as it started, and no amount of effort on my part will ever convince it to become anything else.

Snelling's shoulders slump in defeat, his beard falls limp, even his curlicue mustache seems to tilt the wrong way. Its cobalt-blue tips are now pointing due south. "I don't understand." The words tumble forth in a tone so bereaved I suddenly realize just how much he had riding on this. In his mind, we share this failure equally.

He sucks his lips inward until all that's left of the bottom half of his face is a wilting mustache and a long-bearded chin.

I tug nervously at the stiff white cuffs of my shirtsleeves and loosen the plain black tie looped high at my neck. I'm unable to recall one moment in all my life when I felt worse than this.

"Sir," I begin, determined to turn this around and try to convince him he's still a great teacher, he bears none of the blame.

But before I can finish, his lips pop back into place, and he says, "Grimsly—"

My fingers nervously pluck at the black buttons lining the front of my suit. And while I'm braced for just about anything, mostly I'm hoping he won't mention something about trying again. It's important to know when to quit. Sometimes surrender is the only solution.

"Never forget you have your own unique gifts. Your own duty and purpose." His voice thunders with conviction; his gaze locks on mine. "Some of which you've yet to discover. And as one of Quiver Hollows's most revered and respected citizens, there's absolutely no reason for you to feel bad about ..." He waves a dismissive hand toward the shameful heap of unbent spoons, as though it doesn't matter in the least. While it's nice of him to try to make me feel better, I think we both know the scope of my failure is colossal at best.

A heavy silence descends. I'm desperate to break it, but I can't think of a single word to say that would make this moment any less disappointing for either of us.

Then, just when I'm least expecting it, he breaches the professor-student agreement we stick to whenever I'm in class. For a brief moment he's back to being my trusted guardian who's looked after me since I was an infant.

"Now go." He clutches my shoulder with a heavily bejeweled hand in a way that's meant to be comforting. But considering how I just failed him, his continued kindness only makes me feel worse. "And be quick. You don't want to be late to your own funeral, now, do you?" His eyes twinkle when he says it, and while the joke usually makes me laugh, at the moment I can't even fake it.

Being Quiver Hollows's first, foremost, and only pet funeral director is the one weird thing about me. I used to enjoy all the perks that came with it, namely the way everyone makes such a big deal about me. But the truth is, it's not even that weird. All I do is wear a black suit and come up with the right words to memorialize whatever hamster, goldfish, and/or turtle has recently passed. There are no tails, scales, or supernatural abilities required. It's a made-up weird as opposed to a genuine weird, so it's not like it counts.

"Will you let the next student in? I've got a few more exams still ahead." My guardian's voice pulls me out of my thoughts and back to the present.

He turns away, sending his long blue braid sailing over his shoulder, landing just shy of the bright green sash he wears at his waist. Then he busies himself with straightening his own pile of spoons (no need to straighten mine) as I grasp my bag by the strap and open the door for the next kid in line.

"Hey, Grimsly!" My classmate greets me with the kind of enthusiasm I no longer deserve. "How'd it go? Did you bend all the spoons?" His dark hair is styled the same way as mine, and he's wearing a black suit, white shirt, and black tie with a messenger bag strapped across his chest—same outfit I'm wearing. And believe me, it's not a school uniform, it's just the way I dress. Lately I've noticed a few other kids have taken to copying the look. The kid's face breaks into a grin that sends his whiskers twitching and displays two massive front teeth that protrude way past his lips.

Clearly he looks up to me, so I try to act cool, pretend the outcome wasn't nearly as tragic as I know it to be. But I've never been much good at lying. So it comes as no surprise when I glimpse my reflection in the glass-paneled door and catch myself grimacing. With the absence of any sort of physical oddity, my mop of straight brown hair, somber blue eyes, and full set of unremarkable teeth that fit well within the confines of my mouth pretty much makes me the most boring person around. This kid must be crazy to want to imitate me.

"Can't believe I'm up after you," Rabbit Teeth continues,

stubbornly clinging to a widely held belief that never was true.

I'm not special.

Not gifted.

Not remarkable in any conceivable way.

And as hard as it is to admit, there's no more denying I don't belong in this place.

I heave a deep sigh, take one last look at those wiggling whiskers and shiny white rabbit teeth of his, and push through the door. Squinting into the perpetual haze of fog, clouds, and mist that blankets our town, I wonder, once again, why some people are born so splendidly unique while I'm stuck being boring old me.

TWO

SWEETCRAFT'S CANDY CAVE

I'm the pet funeral director, I remind myself, figuring I could use a good pep talk to make me feel better. *I'm well-known, well-liked. Heck, there are loads of kids who idolize me, dress like me, want to be me . . . though I can't figure out why.*

Maybe it's because Snelling is my guardian, and Snelling is pretty much the most important person in town.

Or maybe it's because of my job and the fact that I've started something that no one ever thought of before.

It could even be because I have a graveyard named after me.

But it's probably mostly due to the fact that, in a town where everyone has some sort of magical or supernatural ability, my complete ordinariness makes me stand out in a really big way.

For the most part, I'm used to it. And while I appreciate how everyone always makes an effort to be encouraging and friendly and make me feel like an important part of the community, what I'd really love more than anything is to go so unnoticed that I completely blend in.

I guess I've just always been different. Which is weird, since I was born and raised here like everyone else. I eat the same food and drink the same water, so I can't help but wonder how it came to be that with all the magic on offer, it somehow managed to bypass me.

To be clear, not everyone around here has rabbit teeth and whiskers or bodies covered in shimmering scales. Two of my closest friends, Ollie and Ming, look more or less normal. But because Ollie could bend spoons practically since birth, and Ming's been levitating since well before she could walk, they're hardly what you'd call ordinary. I'm the only one who can claim that distinction.

All around me the town square pulses with activity. Major preparations are under way for tonight's annual last-day-of-school celebrations, and everyone chatters excitedly about today's final exams.

As usual, I aced all my academic finals last week. But in

a town like this, it's the mystical arts that matter most. Between the fourth-grade tightrope-walking challenge (which I barely passed) and the fifth-grade mind-reading test (which I didn't pass), every year of school has been leading up to Snelling's sixth-grade spoon-bending exam. Those who pass go on to the Manifesters Academy. Those who don't . . . well, no one's ever failed until now.

I know I shouldn't be surprised that I choked. There was not a single sign leading me to believe that I wouldn't. Still, I guess I clung to the hope that, just this once, a little bit of the town's magic would rub off.

Somewhere nearby a boy calls my name. I glance across the road to see a kid with a bright green tail, wearing a messenger bag strapped across his chest, waving excitedly.

"Grimsly! Hey—Grimsly! Over here!" he cries, like I'm someone important—so important he's not just excited to see me, but also for me to see him. "How'd it go on the spoon-bending exam?"

I know he means well, so I take a moment to give a quick wave of acknowledgment before ducking my head and rushing along the cobblestone streets. The last thing I need is to get into a conversation I'm not ready to have.

I race past a long line of misshapen storefronts. Some of them have been left warped by the constant haze of fog, mist, and clouds surrounding our town, while others were purposely made to look that way, with their crooked windows and short, tilted doorways that force most regular-sized people to bend over to enter.

To an outsider, I imagine this place would look as strange as its people. But since we never get any outsiders, I can't say for sure. All I know is I don't allow myself to so much as glance at Sweetcraft's Candy Cave, which is arguably my favorite store.

I'm only a few feet shy of the path that leads home when a very skinny arm slinks around an open doorway as a pair of extra-long fingers latch on to my sleeve.

"Grimsly!" a high-pitched voice cries in greeting. I recognize it as belonging to Mr. Sweetcraft, the owner of the Candy Cave. "Why, you're just in time!"

"In time for what?" I stand my ground outside his shop. I like Mr. Sweetcraft—everyone does—but I have a pet funeral to direct. And since pet funerals are the only thing I seem to be good at, I'm reluctant to miss it.

"To sample my latest creation," he says.

Before I can politely decline, his arm retracts into the store, taking me with it. I find myself deep inside the sparkling cave made entirely of candy.

With its glistening silver walls coated in crystallized sugar and its domed ceiling dotted with brightly colored rock-candy stalactites, this place never fails to amaze me, no matter how many times I visit it.

I follow Mr. Sweetcraft over the small blue bridge that

leads to the other side of the caramel waterfall, which spills into a glimmering white-chocolate pond.

"Help yourself." He extends one of his fingers toward a candied bat hanging upside down from the wall just beside me.

"I'm not one for licorice," I tell him.

"Then you're in luck. It's not made of licorice."

"What is it?" I study the glowing red orbs that stand in for the bat's eyes.

"Top-secret!" Mr. Sweetcraft turns to me with a finger pressed to his lips. His extra-long eyelashes graze his forehead and cheeks with each blink.

"I think I'll go for one of the spiders instead." I pluck a milk-chocolate spider from the wall and pop it into my mouth—only to gasp in surprise when its legs move about on my tongue.

"That's also a new one." He grins. "I call it Scuttle Spider. What do you think?"

It's delicious, no getting around it. Though I have to remind myself it's made of chocolate to force it all the way down.

"Very realistic." I wipe the back of my hand across my lips in an effort to rid myself of the lingering creepy-crawly sensation. I'm just turning to leave when Mr. Sweetcraft's arm springs forward again and grabs hold of me.

"That's not the newest creation," he says. "This is."

He drags me up beside him and presents what looks to be an ordinary piece of bright blue bubble gum. Though nothing in the Candy Cave is ever what it appears to be. And since I've already been lucky enough to try one of the earliest bubble gum offerings, I admit to feeling pretty excited about getting a taste of his latest.

"It works just like the others," he tells me. "Only it's entirely different."

He hands me the piece and without hesitation I take it.

"Chew it up real good." He watches excitedly. "Then, when it's ready, when the gum is thoroughly softened and workable, blow the biggest bubble your lungs will allow."

I work my jaw hard. Last time I tried one of these, Mr. Sweetcraft gave me a yellow piece. When I blew it into a bubble, a lime-green frog appeared on the inside and hopped around. That was until Mr. Sweetcraft popped the bubble with a rock-candy stalactite and the frog leaped free. I spent the next ten minutes picking pieces of gum from my clothing and cheeks.

"Still working out the kinks on that last bit of messiness," he'd said, helping me clean myself up.

According to my friends, each color represents a different surprise. The pink piece comes with a pair of glasses hidden inside that allow you to reexperience favorite moments of your life. The purple has a deck of cards that shuffle and deal themselves. So I can hardly wait to see what this blue one will offer.

"Ready?" He claps his hands excitedly.

I flatten the gum against the roof of my mouth, then push it down the front and stretch it a bit with the tip of my tongue.

"Easy does it. . . ." Mr. Sweetcraft holds his breath and watches me closely.

Slowly, I blow into the gum. With my gaze nearly cross-eyed, I watch it expand.

"Just a little more," he coaxes.

Though I'm not sure how much more I can go. The bubble is nearly touching the floor now, and from what I can tell, it's empty.

"I don't . . . I don't understand." Mr. Sweetcraft glances between the bubble and me. "I've run plenty of tests. This has never happened before. Not once. Not ever."

I'm not sure what to do. I've got a giant-sized bubble with no prize inside attached to my face.

Do I pop it?

Try to reel it back in?

I look to Mr. Sweetcraft for help, but he's too caught up in the despair of his bubble gum failure.

"It always works. It never fails. Every test I've done—and believe me, I've done plenty—has ended successfully."

I nod that I understand while still pleading with my eyes for some sort of guidance on how to proceed.

"I just can't explain it." His shock of orange hair wilts against his cheeks. His slim shoulders slump in defeat. With a weary shake of his head, he jabs a pin into the bubble, and I watch it disappear as though it was never there.

"Well, you perfected that part," I tell him, though I'm not sure he heard. He's too mired in grief over his failed candy experiment. "I don't think you should give up on it. I think you should try it again. Maybe that was just a bum piece."

My attempt to make him feel better doesn't seem to penetrate. So I let myself out and head for the path that leads home. I wonder if I should've said something about failing my exam. Maybe that failure somehow (I don't know how, but somehow) affected the bubble gum's performance. Like failure can multiply or something.

I'm making my way through the park, enjoying the way the perpetual veil of mist swirls and dips as my arms and legs cut through it, when I notice a group of people clustered around the area known as Chilling Cove. They're gathered too tightly for me to see what they're so excited about.

On any other day, I wouldn't hesitate to investigate. But after the unexpected detour into the Candy Cave, I have no time to spare. Like Snelling joked: I really don't want to be late for my own funeral. And though I do feel bad for the grieving, I have to admit I am looking forward to doing the one thing I seem to be good at on this otherwise not-so-good day.

In my rush to get away, I could almost swear I hear someone cry: "Chilling Cove is boiling over!" But I'm quick to dismiss it.

Chilling Cove is chilled. That's just the way it's always been.

Just like Pendulum Falls flows in a loop, and some people are born with pointy elf ears and spoon-bending skills.

Anything else is completely implausible.

A failed spoon-bending exam and a bum piece of gum do not mean the world is coming to an end.

I shake away the thought and race toward home. I have a pet funeral to officiate. Everything else can be sorted out later.

THREE

DEARLY DEPARTED GOLDFISH

Dearly beloved, we are gathered here today to celebrate the surprisingly long and memorable life of Mr. Wiggles the goldfish. As a black moor goldfish, Mr. Wiggles was best known for his velvety dark color, his telescoping eyes, his poor vision, and his slow swimming style, which made it look as though he was wiggling through his fish tank. That's how he got his name. . . .

My voice drones on, the words flowing easily as my mind begins to drift. As far as eulogies go, it's pretty standard stuff. But now, after failing the spoon-bending exam, the memorial takes on more meaning than any before. Since directing pet funerals is the only thing I seem to be good at—the only thing that distinguishes me from everyone else—I feel the need to give this one my all.

Due to his slow swimming style, Mr. Wiggles was often the last in the aquarium to reach the food. Luckily, he had Albie watching over him. As soon as Albie noticed the problem, he moved Mr. Wiggles to his own tank, where he thrived, and even outlived his former tank mates by several years. . . .

I catch sight of Albie. His protruding, goldfish-like eyes are streaming with tears, just like they were when he approached me about giving Mr. Wiggles a proper goodbye.

"I feel like I've lost a brother," he'd said. "Maybe even a twin. Will you help me?"

Of course I agreed. I always do. Though it's strange to think how what started as a onetime thing when I lost my pet mouse, Merlin, back when I was eight, has turned into the thing I'm now known for.

Albie's shaky fingers awkwardly clutch at the tiny fish-shaped coffin. He sniffles so loudly that I pluck my handkerchief from my pocket and offer it to him without missing a beat.

. . . And so, Mr. Wiggles, we thank you for all the joy you've brought to the lives of those fortunate enough to have known you, and for now, we bid you farewell. Goodbye, old friend—until we meet again!

I give a subtle nod toward the band, and the horn section

breaks into a slow, mournful tune. Then I take the box from Albie and place it into the small hole I dug earlier this morning when I cut through Summerfield Lawn on my way to school. Albie kneels down to scoop up a handful of soil to toss onto Mr. Wiggles's grave. And when the rest of the mourners step forward to do the same, I can't help but notice how many of them are dressed just like me.

A teenage girl, her legs covered in shimmering iridescent scales, pulls a bag of fish flakes from her messenger bag and sprinkles some on top of the dirt before handing the bag to the boy right beside her. He fumbles to grasp it securely in his extra-large lobster-claw hands with the outside fingers fused together and the middle finger missing.

The boy turns and looks at me, and I struggle to place him. With his hood pulled down so it hangs low over his forehead, half of his face is concealed. A moment later, Albie says, "How soon can I get a new one?" and the boy with the unusual hands is all but forgotten.

Albie wipes his palms down the front of his pants and looks at me with those large, round, watery eyes that bulge out at the sides. "I mean, no disrespect to Mr. Wiggles, but the thing is, I've always had a fish. I've never not had a fish. And so I'm kind of eager to, you know, replace him." He casts a guilty look toward his beloved pet's final resting place. "But do you think it's too soon?"

Part of being a pet funeral director involves listening,

sympathizing, and sometimes doling out advice to the grieving. It's a part of the job I take very seriously.

I run a hand over my tie, maneuvering it until it falls neatly down the long row of buttons on my shirt. Then I look at him and say, "I don't see the problem. I think Mr. Wiggles would understand your need for a new fish friend."

The boy wipes his eyes and starts to walk away, only to turn back a moment later and say, "Oh, I almost forgot—here." He retrieves a small box from his pocket and hands it to me. "It's from Mr. Wiggles's aquarium." He nods at the No Fishing sign I find tucked inside. "I wanted you to have it. Out of all the decorations, he liked that one the best. He had a pretty good sense of humor for a fish."

I watch him go as I slip the sign into the inside pocket of my suit jacket. Later I'll add it to the growing pile of leashes, balls, chew toys, and hamster wheels—the shrine of mementos from all the pets that have passed on since I started this service three years ago. And for one brief moment, I wonder if maybe my failure isn't nearly as bad as I think.

Maybe Snelling is right.

Maybe I really do have other gifts that are lying dormant for now but will soon be revealed.

Besides, it's not like Snelling's going to tell anyone about how I choked on my final. So maybe, just maybe, no one will ever find out.

"We know about the test."

I turn to find Ming staring down at me from under the line of straight dark bangs that cuts across her forehead. Her ballet slipper–clad feet (the only type of shoes I've ever seen her wear) hover a few inches above the ground.

Penelope stands silently beside her. With her pale skin and blue-velvet-and-lace dress, she looks almost ghostlike as she twirls a clump of curly red hair round and round her index finger. Her eyes—one blue, one green—fix on mine.

"We know all about it," Ming continues, and when I catch the look on her face, the way her dark eyes narrow, the way her mouth turns down, I realize I've been fooling myself. Secrets are impossible to keep in a small town populated by very odd people with preternatural abilities.

"Ignore her." Ollie frowns at Ming, then looks encouragingly at me. "You okay, Grimsly?" he asks.

As a direct descendant of Yegor Quiver, Ollie inherited his great-great-grandfather's wild, wavy blond hair, dark eyes, and olive skin. And according to Ollie's mom, he exhibited an amazing gift for spoon bending practically from birth. Every time she tried to feed him, he'd distort the spoon so the food would end up in her lap instead of his mouth.

He looks at me, waiting for a response, as Penelope and Ming lean in.

But the truth is, I don't know what to say. They're my

best friends, so I know they mean well, but that doesn't make this any easier.

With Ollie's superior spoon-bending skills (he can easily bend two piles of spoons in less than the one minute required), Ming's ballet-like levitating (she doesn't just hover, she spins and twirls and does jaw-dropping grand jetés that she can hold for a really long time), and Penelope's elfin ears and talent for telepathy, they're all so weird in such amazing ways, there's just no way they could understand what it's like to be boring and normal like me.

Pretty much everyone assumes Ollie will replace Professor Snelling one day and teach the next generation of spoon benders. And while I'm happy for him and know it only makes sense, somehow I guess I always hoped the job would be passed on to me.

It probably sounds crazy since I'm not related to Snelling, but since my real parents are gone, he's the closest thing to a father I've ever known. My mom died during childbirth, which has always made me feel guilty, like I'm somehow to blame, even though Snelling assures me I'm not. Then, just two years later, my father died of a broken heart—literally. He was so despondent over the loss of my mother, his heart simply stopped working.

According to Snelling, he found me crawling around Summerfield Lawn surrounded by a fluffle of multicolored bunnies. He had no idea how I'd gotten there, but he was determined to help me move on from my tragic past. Without hesitation, he stepped up to raise me, and I've been watching him bend stuff with his mind ever since.

Heck, I grew up in the biggest twisted-wood-and-metal house in this town. So considering all that, I'd have thought at least some of his talent would've transferred to me.

Clearly I was wrong.

"I saw it," Penelope says, the sound of her voice startling me. She's a telepath, so her vocabulary is extremely limited. It's not often she actually speaks.

"She's starting to get visions," Ming says, by way of explanation. "And she had one of you."

"I can speak for myself." Penelope rolls one blue eye as the green one holds steady. "I had a vision," she repeats, failing to supply anything more, which sets Ming into hysterics, which makes Penelope scowl.

"What sort of vision?" I ask. "You mean like remote viewing—like you were spying on me from afar?" My mind reels with the implications of this new revelation. We all agreed, a long time ago, that mind reading between friends was strictly off-limits for obvious reasons. But a remote viewer—someone able to view events without actually being there—could be even worse. Up until now my friends couldn't do that, but is it possible Penelope has developed that skill?

"Relax." Ming shoots a cautious look at Penelope before she continues. "It's not what you think."

"No one's reading anyone's minds," Ollie assures me. "You know how she can communicate mentally, with both words and pictures, but mainly in pictures?" He jabs a thumb toward Penelope.

I shrug. Having no supernatural abilities, I wouldn't know for sure. I've never been able to receive one of Penelope's brain paintings like everyone else. But since they've all assured me they're amazing, I just go along and assume it was true.

"Well, now she's receiving pictures out of the blue," Ming says. "And even though she's not sure where they come from, I was there when it happened, and—"

"And we weren't sure it was true until we just now saw you." Ollie finishes the thought for her.

"She saw an image of your face—like an oil painting, a portrait," Ming translates for Penelope. "Your eyes were dark and hollow, your mouth was turned down, and you looked so sad, so lost, and . . . well, you looked just like you do now."

"Um, okay." I stare down at my feet, since I'm too humiliated to look directly at my friends.

"So, what now?" Ollie asks.

"Will you have to repeat the sixth grade?" Ming frowns at the thought, though I'm not sure if that's because they'll all be leaving me behind or because in the history of Quiver

Hollows it's never happened before. And no matter how hard I try to convince myself it doesn't matter, there's just no denying it does. It matters a lot.

"I'm sure Snelling will let you take it again if you ask him," Ollie tries to reassure me.

"I don't want to take it again," I tell him. "There's no point. I'm not like you. I'm not like anyone here. There's absolutely nothing odd or unusual or supernatural about me."

My friends fall quiet. Then Ming asks, "How did Snelling handle it?" Her tone is softer, hesitant, as opposed to her usual bluster, which shows just how much she pities me. "What did he say?"

I remember the look of despair on Snelling's face, but it's too painful to talk about, so I shake my head and wave the question away. "I have no idea what happens next. No one does. Even in a town built on magic, not a single one of us can see into the future."

"Well …" Ming's feet flutter in place as she levitates high above our heads and grins in her usual enigmatic way. "There's one person who *can* see into the future. Maybe it's time we go find her."

FOUR

NO QUIVER, NO SHAKE

"Him," Ollie says.

"What?" Ming immediately drops to the ground, sending her pink-feathered dress fluttering around. Her feet land in first position, with her toes turned outward, heels touching.

"If you're talking about the Seer, then the Seer is a *him*," Ollie states, his tone ringing with the kind of authority that, if you didn't know better, you'd think he'd actually met the Seer. But I'm willing to bet he hasn't. Nobody has.

Penelope shoots a meaningful look at Ollie and Ming,

then reaches up to pluck a purple-and-white-striped orchid from a stem that's looped around a tree limb.

"She says that the Seer is nothing and everything." Ming squints at Penelope before continuing. "The Seer is whatever you perceive the Seer to be."

Penelope tucks the bloom behind her own ear and grins.

"I don't understand." Ming frowns.

"For good luck." Penelope gestures to the flower.

"No." Ming shakes her head. "About the Seer. I don't get it. How is it possible for something to be nothing and everything?"

Penelope shrugs.

"It's just how the legend goes." Ollie grows quiet, as though he's mulling it over.

I stand alongside my friends, not even bothering to contribute to the conversation. I've already decided the whole thing is moot. I'm not going to see the Seer, so none of it matters.

For one thing, I'm not even sure I believe there is a Seer.

For another, why would I want to know the future? From where I stand in this present moment, it looks pretty grim. So why would I want to get bad news ahead of time? It would be like living it twice.

"Well, I've never heard that legend before." Ming is back to hovering again. "I've heard lots of legends, but not that one."

I should speak up. Say something to stop this dumb argument. But while they're busy focusing on the Seer, they're not focusing on my failure, or at least not directly. So I choose to remain quiet and wait for them to grow bored with the topic and move on to another.

"I'm not even sure there's any truth to the legend," Ollie says. "I don't know anyone who's actually seen the Seer. Then again, if all the stuff about the path being filled with twisted, vicious, flesh-eating plants is true, then it's entirely possible the Seer doesn't exactly want to be seen."

Penelope folds her arms across her chest and frowns. Ollie looks at me and says, "Penelope just sent us a picture of a large door with a sign that says *Do Not Disturb!* She says no one likes an unexpected visitor."

"But what if the flesh-eating plants are only put there as a test?" As usual, Ming refuses to give in until she's argued every angle. "What if you have to earn the right to see the Seer, and once you've survived, you're in?" Her dark eyes brighten when she looks at me, like she can't wait to send me off on a quest that I may or may not return from, just to see if her theory was right.

Before this can go any further, I say, "Guys—look, I know you want to help, but I'm not going to see the Seer. I don't want to know if the legends are true. What if it turns out they are? Why would I want to put myself through that kind of horror? It's too dangerous, too risky. It's easier to talk to

Snelling instead. Between the two of us, we'll figure out a way to go forward. Besides—"

At that moment, the town bells set to ringing, and we all brace for the daily six o'clock trembler that lasts exactly twenty-six seconds and doesn't result in any real damage unless you're on a ladder or something. Hence the sixteen-second warning.

Only this time, the earth doesn't quake.

And after about a full minute of stunned silence, where even Ming is too startled to speak, Ollie ventures a timid "Did—did anyone feel anything?" His brown eyes widen and his blond hair stands on end as he tries to make sense of what truly just happened, or rather, failed to happen.

"Not a thing," Ming says, but then, seeing as how her feet weren't even touching the ground, of course she didn't.

"Me neither," I say as Penelope shakes her head.

"What do you think it means?" I wonder aloud, overcome with a deep sense of dread.

Quiver Hollows may be weird, but it's consistent. There's no such thing as a fluke. I was born and raised in this place, and I can't remember a single day when the earth didn't quake.

I catch sight of Professor Snelling rushing up the walkway so fast he's like a blur of swirling silk robes, purple slippers, and tangled white beard.

"Grimsly!" His voice is harsh, his manner is hurried, and

his cobalt-tipped curlicue mustache is skewed the worst I've ever seen it. "Come inside at once!" Then, noticing Penelope, Ming, and Ollie, he adds, "All of you, hurry home! And quickly! Tonight's festivities have been canceled. I'm sure your parents are waiting!"

Before I can even say goodbye to my friends, Snelling has grabbed me by the elbow and whisked me inside. He plunks me onto the sofa and paces nervously, all the while talking to himself.

I strain to hear, but he's mumbling in a way that I can't make out the words.

"Sir—sir, what is it?" I venture, addressing him more formally than I normally would, but then nothing about today feels like any other day that came before.

I'm the first person in Quiver Hollows to fail the sixth-grade spoon-bending exam.

Mr. Sweetcraft's latest bubble gum offering didn't work.

A group of people claimed that Chilling Cove was boiling over.

The six o'clock tremor was a no-show.

And now, according to Snelling, the annual last-day-of-school celebrations are canceled.

It's enough to put me on edge.

Snelling stops in front of the hearth, rubs his palms together, then turns to me and says, "Something very serious is happening."

My hands twist nervously in my lap as I wait for him to continue.

"I'm sure you noticed that the earth failed to shake. Not so much as a quiver."

I nod, not daring to speak. Until now, I always thought it was funny how Quiver Hollows actually quivers, without fail, every day (except for today), seeing as how the town was named in honor of the world-famous explorer Yegor Quiver. According to legend, Yegor was both magic-minded and pure of heart, which is exactly how he came to find this place when the rest of the world doesn't even know we exist. (And from what we know about the rest of the world, we're good with that.) It was the kind of synchronicity that always amused me, but now, on the day the earth failed to shake, it's starting to seem a little more sinister.

I try to remain calm, but Snelling's taking such an agonizingly long time to explain I can't help but fidget.

"And while it may please you to know that you are not the only one to fail the spoon-bending exam—"

What?

I sit up straighter, wanting to ask him to repeat what he just said, but knowing better, I choose to replay the words in my head. And while I know it's not right, or kind, I have to admit that discovering I'm not the only one who choked really does make me feel better.

"There were seventeen students who took the exam after you. All of them flunked."

Wait—what?

Seventeen kids—and all of them failures like me?

It's too much to be a coincidence. Something more is going on here.

I think of the rabbit-toothed, whisker-faced kid who was next in line, remembering how he dressed like me, how nervous he was about going after me, wrongly assuming I set the bar too high for him to reach. Did I somehow infect him, or jinx him in some way without even realizing?

I focus on Snelling and try to catch up with what he's been saying.

"At first I thought it was me." Snelling's long talons sink into his beard, raking and twisting in the sort of slow repetitive motion I find almost hypnotizing. "Maybe it's time I retire, I thought. Maybe I'm not the teacher I once was."

I start to protest, but the searching look he shoots me keeps the words from escaping.

"But then . . ." He turns back toward the stone hearth, as though the answers we seek are kept in the ashes of last night's fire. "I passed by Pendulum Falls on my way home . . ."

My stomach begins to twist and knot. Already I can tell this particular story has no happy ending.

". . . and Pendulum Falls no longer flows in a loop."

I'm dumbstruck. Gobsmacked. I can't even imagine such a thing.

Responding to the confused look on my face, Snelling spells it out for me. "It's flowing *normally*. Spilling from the top to the bottom without looping back up again."

I suck in a breath. The horrifying image blooms in my head—it feels like the end of everything I once knew about our world.

"What's happening? What's causing this normalcy?" Not knowing what else to say, I go for the obvious.

It takes Snelling a long time to reply, but when he does, his gaze is weary beyond his years. "I don't know." His lids droop as he seems to retreat into himself. "I can't be sure."

"But—" I prod for more. I can tell he's got something important to add, but for whatever reason, he hesitates. And while I'm not entirely sure I'm ready to hear it, I'm pretty sure he's overreacting. Surely there's a way to explain all this.

He opens his eyes and sets himself squarely before me. "It's possible that the very magic that has bound this place for so long is now . . ."

His fingers begin braiding his beard, which is never a good sign. I try my best to just let the story unfold at Snelling's own natural, excruciatingly slow pace. The wait is testing every part of my being.

". . . Well, it's quite possible, or at least there's a very good chance, that with the loss of magic—if there is a loss of magic, which there very definitely seems to be—well, with that in mind, it means that our town, our beloved Quiver Hollows, is rapidly normalizing. Which is to say that it's becoming like everywhere else. Which would explain all the failed exams, Pendulum Falls, and the absence of today's tremor."

"Okay," I say, refusing to believe it. "So a bunch of us failed a spoon-bending exam, and the earth forgot to shake, and the waterfall has stopped looping." I pause for a breath, realizing I purposely left out the part about Chilling Cove boiling over and Mr. Sweetcraft's failed bubble gum. I see no reason to add to the already-long list. "Is that really a good enough reason to jump to such a drastic conclusion? That our nonperfect utopia is becoming just like the very world we've done our best to avoid? I mean, what if Quiver Hollows is simply having a bad day?"

According to the defeated slant of Snelling's shoulders and the downward tilt of his chin, my little rant resulted in nothing more than an unnecessary release of hot air into the room.

"Grimsly, there are no bad days in Quiver Hollows."

That's all he says.

It's all he needs to say.

Until today, Quiver Hollows has always been a happy, friendly, extremely odd place where people of all different sorts lived in harmony, and our strange daily occurrences hummed along without so much as a glitch.

The truth hangs heavy, and we both seem to sag under its weight. And yet I won't give up on the need to set things right, or at least the need to set them right in my head.

"W-well, okay, m-maybe," I stutter. "I mean, yes. Yes. Clearly you're right. There are no bad days here, and everything you mentioned is alarming, for sure. But what if it's just a blip? I mean, what if it's not as big a deal as we think? Maybe if we just let the day run its course, then tomorrow, everything will be back to being weird again. If normal things are happening, then there must be some sort of logical explanation!"

It all sounded so good in my head, but the execution doesn't have the effect I hoped. The look Snelling gives me is so pained, I find myself cringing under his gaze.

"Yes, Grimsly," he says, his tone grave. "But what I haven't been able to tell you is that, according to many in town, the reason is you."

FIVE

BAD INFLUENCE

"Me?"

I leap from the sofa, but now that I'm up, I'm not sure what to do, so I repeat what I already said.

"Seriously, *me?* How can that be?"

But then it hits me. The words are barely out of my mouth when I totally understand what he's getting at.

Of course it's me!

Why wouldn't it be me?

After all, I'm the only normal one here. In a town full of weird, my absolute ordinariness makes me stand out. Just think about all the attention I get from the little kids who look up to me, who admire me, and who try their best to be like me. They've taken to wearing black suits and strapping a messenger bag across their chests. And since everyone knows that the things you focus on have a way of becoming real—it only makes sense!

"Ever since you gave me Summerfield Lawn to look after and turn into the pet cemetery, everyone's turned their focus on me." The words spill forth before I have a chance to try them out first in my head. But I don't need to. I'm right. And there's no doubt in my mind that I'm on to something. "I knew this was bad all along. The kids all think I'm so cool, with my black suits and having a graveyard named after me, that they've even started to emulate me. They're actually trying to become boring and normal, and it's working. Only it's working too well, since everyone knows that young magic is the most potent magic. So in their attempt to become normal and boring like me, they're turning Quiver Hollows normal and boring too!" Once the truth has a chance to sink in, it doesn't feel nearly as good as I assumed it would.

Sometimes being right isn't all it's cracked up to be. Especially when my being right means that I'm infecting the town, no matter how unintentionally.

"No, Grimsly," Snelling says, but it's a halfhearted protest at best.

"The kid with the whiskers and rabbit teeth failed because he was so worried about going after me he lost his confidence." I don't even know why I'm saying what I'm saying. Why I insist on continuing to build a case against myself. But I'm on a roll, and there's no stopping me until I've dug my own grave. "And then once he failed, there was a domino effect, resulting in seventeen failures and more."

"I'm not entirely sure that's the case—" Another dispirited attempt from Snelling that I quickly interrupt before it can go any further.

"Of course it's the case—there's no other way to explain it! Everyone in Quiver Hollows is unique—everyone but me. And their delusional quest for normalcy is wrecking everything that once made this town great!"

Snelling stands before me, his face haggard and grieved. He once seemed so timeless, but now his one-hundred-plus years are starting to show. "There's something I've been meaning to tell you," he says. "A conversation I should not have delayed—"

Before he can breathe another word, the evening edition of the *Quiver Hollows Herald* shoots through the mail slot in the front door and skids to a stop at his purple slipper–clad feet. The two of us stare in disbelief at the headline screaming across the front page:

LABRADOR RETRIEVER
GIVES BIRTH TO LITTER OF PUPS—
ALL LABS!
NOT A SINGLE PURPLE
PIGLET AMONG THEM!

Just below the headline is a picture of the mama nursing her pups—an image that would normally be considered charming and cute if it weren't so incredibly alarming.

Snelling and I exchange a look, and before he can stop me, I'm running out the front door.

SIX

SIX FEET UNDER

Just to be clear, the dramatic exit is far more effective when you actually have a clearheaded plan and a definite destination in mind.

Running out the door just for the sake of doing so—or, in my case, because you can't stand to be inside with yourself, only to discover that you also can't stand to be outside with yourself—doesn't really yield the sort of result you might think.

To his credit, Snelling doesn't follow. Not that I expected he would. Although, if I'm going to be honest, then I might as well admit that part of me kind of wanted him to. While there's nothing he could actually say or do that would alter the horrifying truth—that the townspeople blame me for Quiver Hollows losing its magic and becoming as boring and normal as everywhere else—the moment I found myself alone under the perpetual dome of fog, clouds, and mist, well, I wasn't entirely sure I was up for my own company.

But since I'm not quite ready to go back inside, I decide to wander instead. Making my way to the back of the property, I stand beneath the twisted metal arch that reads SUMMERFIELD LAWN and fiddle with the puzzle lock on the gate Snelling made to divide his house from the graveyard. (There's no crime in Quiver Hollows, so there's no reason to lock anyone out—but Snelling loves to bend metal as much as he loves a good puzzle, so he includes secret latches and riddles in nearly every item he makes.)

Once I let myself through, I take in the expanse of turquoise-tinged lawn that yields to the collection of elaborate headstones. The markers vary in size, but all of them serve to memorialize the beloved pets that have passed on and been laid to rest. There's a tiny wooden hamster wheel that spins whenever a breeze picks up. There's also a towering replica of a cat condo, its multiple cubbies and perches decorated with brightly colored flowers and vines. And while I can't help but feel a momentary sense of pride for being the one to honor so many lives on such a grand scale, I'm also overcome with regret for the showy sort of manufactured life I've created for myself and the devastating effects it's now wrought on this town.

I walk among the headstones, stopping before the one I designed for Merlin, my beloved pet mouse, who once lived inside the pocket of my T-shirt (back when I still wore T-shirts). With Ming's and Penelope's input, I sketched my idea on a notepad; then we all stood back and watched as Ollie—using only his mind and a few pieces of donated scrap metal—managed to create a perfect replica of an extra-large T-shirt with a mouse peeking out of the pocket, just like I'd drawn.

I was only eight at the time and had no real memory of losing my parents, so Merlin's loss felt like too much to bear. I moped around our strange twisted-wood-and-metal house, thinking about how much I missed having him around. It wasn't long before Snelling took me for a walk in Summerfield Lawn and told me I could do with it whatever I wanted. The only catch being that I had to use it for something more productive and useful than feeling sorry for myself.

I gazed out at the wide and glimmering field—the place I'd always been drawn to, the place where Snelling first found me. When I shared my idea to turn it into a pet cemetery so I could give Merlin, and other pets like him, the sort of grand send-offs their lives deserved, well . . . for a moment, Snelling looked deeply disturbed.

His expression grew serious, his posture tense and still. And when he did speak, it seemed as though he had to force the words past his lips.

"Grimsly." He placed his hands on my shoulders and looked me square in the face in an effort to convey the high-level of seriousness of whatever came next. "While I can't say I'm surprised by your choice, I will agree on one condition. . . ."

I held my breath until it felt like it might burst through my cheeks. For every second of anticipation, I found my longing for the pet cemetery increasing. And yet, as I held Snelling's gaze, there was no denying the silent war he had waging inside.

"You must promise to protect the bones at any cost."

I gave a quick nod, rubbed my lips together, and waited for more.

And there was more. I could tell by the way his lips trembled with unspoken words.

But instead, he just ruffled my hair and mumbled something about there being plenty of time to continue the conversation later. Then he switched the topic to the gate he would design to honor the place.

While Snelling went to work on the gate, I went out and scored my first black suit and wrote my first eulogy. It wasn't long before everyone in town started asking me to memorialize their pets whenever they were unfortunate enough to lose one.

Before I knew it, directing pet funerals had become my weird thing. And I'm not gonna lie: it felt good to finally have a thing—something that made me valuable, unique, and most importantly, odd.

And yeah, the first time I saw some kid trying to emulate me, I thought it was cool. It's only now that I realize I should've put a stop to it. Should never have let it get to this point.

I reach into my pocket and fumble with the No Fishing sign Albie gave me earlier today, back when I thought failing the spoon-bending exam was the worst of my problems. But with hindsight comes clarity, as they say, and now that the worst has happened, I know just what to do to set things right and make sure it never happens again.

I turn back toward the house, ready to confide in Snelling all about my new plan. How I'm going to turn things around by packing up my black suits, shutting down the pet funeral business, and then spending the next several months staying out of sight.

Before Summerfield Lawn opened for business, most people (aside from my friends) paid me no notice. But now it's become clear that over the course of the last three years, there's been far too much attention directed my way. And slowly, surely, it's draining the town of everything that once made it such an exceptional place.

It's time for the townspeople to return their focus to the

kinds of things that really matter, like magic, individuality, and keeping Quiver Hollows weird.

I pick up the pace, in a hurry to explain my plan to Snelling, imagining the flood of relief that will wash across his face as he agrees wholeheartedly with everything I say—

Without warning, the toe of my right shoe smashes hard into a mound of dirt, and before I can stop it, I'm stumbling.

Falling.

Slipping through space with my arms windmilling wildly, uselessly, unable to keep the inevitable from happening.

I hit the ground hard. So hard I can feel my insides rattle, my brain scramble. It takes a moment before I get my bearings and realize that the strange metallic-tasting liquid seeping into my mouth is actually a stream of blood pouring out of my nostrils.

I reach for my handkerchief, but then I remember I gave it to Albie earlier today. I use the end of my tie to sop up the mess, hoping my nose is merely hurt and not broken. Then I reach into my pocket and retrieve my penlight. I flip the switch and discover I've fallen into Chauncey the pony's grave.

In life, Chauncey had a beautiful flowing golden mane, a swishing silver tail, and a sparkly purple unicorn horn that peeked out from under his blue forelock.

In death—well, Chauncey's no longer here.

Someone has dug up the grave and left a severed hand in the place where pony bones should be.

At the sight of it, I jump!

Scream!

And the next thing I know, the whole world turns black.

SEVEN

PONY BONES

A handful of terrified moments later, I calm down just enough to realize that the whole world didn't actually go black.

Rather, the coffin lid slammed shut so quickly that it startled me and I accidentally hit the switch on my penlight and made it seem like it had.

And with that in mind, I figure it's also safe to assume that what I mistook for a severed hand wasn't actually a severed hand at all. In my panicked, dazed, and bloody-nosed state, I only imagined it was.

With a shaky grip, I pry open the coffin lid and aim the

narrow beam toward the place where I thought I saw a severed hand only to confirm that yes, it really *is* a severed hand,
and I start to scream all over again.

I bolt to the far edge of the grave, push hard against the
towering wall of dirt at my back, and fight to get ahold of
myself when really, there's no chance of that. I mean, I'm
trapped in a grave with a severed hand and I have no idea
how any of this could've happened.

Graves don't just un-dig themselves.

Pony skeletons don't just evaporate into thin air.

Hands don't just randomly fall off wrists.

Even in a weird town like this, none of those scenarios
makes any sense.

*Okay. You need to calm down. You need to relax just enough
so that you can come up with a better way to handle this. Everyone knows that wisdom never results from panic.*

I force my eyes closed and begin a slow countdown from
ten. By the time I reach one, I'm just settled enough to confidently pop one eye open and confirm, yet again, that yes, it
is indeed a severed hand.

Only it's a fake hand.

More like a glove, really, or even an extra-large oven mitt.

What gave it away were the rubber edges and the absence of the sort of blood and gore you might expect to see
when stumbling upon a severed hand.

Though in my defense, at first sight it really does

resemble the real thing. And with a long sleeve pulled down low enough to cover the wrist, well, pretty much anyone would've been fooled.

I know I was when I saw the boy wearing that very same hand at Mr. Wiggles's funeral just a few hours before.

With the middle finger missing and the outer fingers fused together on either side, it looks like a lobster claw, which made it hard for the boy to handle the bag of fish feed when the girl with shimmering blue scales passed it his way.

I remember how he turned to look at me—how I struggled to place him. But then Albie started talking and I never saw the boy again.

But he was here.

And he stole Chauncey's bones and left this fake lobster-claw hand in their place.

Clearly he wants me to know it was him. Leaving the hand behind was no accident.

But why?

And what could he possibly want with the bones from a dead pony?

EIGHT

TORCHES AND PITCHFORKS

When I finally climb out of the grave, nighttime has come. I manage to find my way back to the house thanks to the ceiling of twinkling lights that Snelling strewed around the property.

Because of the perpetual dome of fog, clouds, and mist that covers the town, direct sunlight never manages to find its way in. And with the absence of the moon and stars and anything else that might normally light up the sky from afar, darkness tends to fall as black and infinite as a void.

Carefully, I pick my way toward the house. My nose still

aches from my fall, but I'm so eager to share my idea for making Quiver Hollows odd again, the deep, throbbing pain takes a backseat to everything else.

Though I do hope Snelling's not mad about the pony bones. It was my job to protect them. I promised I would. But now that they're missing, it's yet another failure to add to the list.

The first things I notice when I let myself through the gate is an unexpected halo of flickering lights and the lilt of several voices all speaking at once.

I sigh in relief, taking it as a sign that the last-day-of-school celebrations are back on. The voices probably belong to my classmates and friends. I bet they've been waiting for me to return so we can enjoy the festivities together.

Clearly things aren't nearly as bad as I thought.

Life as I know it is about to get right back on track.

I rush toward the house, eager to see Snelling and my friends. I'm just nearing the back when I hear a crowd of people scream things like:

"Failed the exam and now I can't bend a spoon, either—none of us can!"

"So much for my telepathy, never mind my clairvoyant abilities—how am I supposed to communicate with my poor deceased cat?"

"Haven't been able to manifest a thing—how are we supposed to feed and clothe everyone without magic?"

"No piglets—just puppies—it's an atrocity!"

"Chilling Cove is boiling over!"

"It rained—actually rained—for a full five minutes directly over my house!"

"Well, you think that's bad? The sun shone all over me, and I have the sunburn to prove it!"

"Yeah, well, the scales are falling right off my kid's body and nothing—nothing—will put them back on!"

This is not what I thought.

It's bad.

Really bad.

Still, I continue. There must be something I can do or say to calm them. I'm in the middle of planning the speech in my head, when one unsettling voice rises above all the others:

"Where's Grimsly? Bring him to us! We know you're hiding him, and you know as well as we do that he's responsible for all this! We've tolerated him for long enough, but no more! As the Keeper, he was supposed to keep this from happening. But now it's clear the boy bears the same curse as his family, and it's infecting us all!"

In an instant, I dash toward the side of the house where no one can see me—my head spinning with all I just heard.

They called me the Keeper—the Keeper of what, exactly? What does he mean? No one ever told me I was the Keeper.

And what was that about a family curse? Snelling's the only family I've ever known, and while I know we're not even related, he never once mentioned anything about my real family being cursed.

The crowd grows louder, angrier, and I watch from the shadows as they join together with their own impromptu chant:

"His curse is a disease, and now it's time for Grimsly to leave!"

Like the worst sort of earworm, it really catches on, and it's only a matter of moments before everyone is singing my least favorite song.

The glare of torches turns their angry faces to a sickening shade of orange, and though Snelling does his best to calm them, his words fall on deaf ears. These people are furious, fearful, and fueled by paranoia. They don't want well-considered assurances or a plan that makes sense. They want knee-jerk reactions and drastic, impulsive, high-risk solutions. Anything that will make it appear—however briefly—that all is right in their world.

And suddenly it becomes clear that the only way to help Snelling—the only way to repay him for all he's done—is to go somewhere very far away, just like the crowd said.

While Snelling continues in vain to restore a sense of order and reason, I sneak through the back door, grab my messenger bag, strap it across my chest, and run back out again.

And though I'm saddened I didn't have enough time to leave a goodbye note, at least this time I know exactly where I'm headed, for better or worse.

NINE

INTO THE WOODS

I run all the way to the mouth of the woods before I finally take a moment to stop and catch my breath. I maybe even spend a few seconds trying to convince myself that I don't really have to do this.

That it's not as bad as I think.

That I'm completely overreacting.

But when I pull my regular flashlight from my bag and shine it on the stream—the same stream that used to flow in a lovely shade of rainbow that's now a murky, bleak, foul-smelling, stagnant pool of muck—there's no more pretending that our beloved town is not under some kind of horribly normal siege.

I assumed it was because of the way all the kids have begun to imitate me.

The angry mob outside Snelling's house claimed it's because I'm the Keeper and my family is cursed.

Even though I have no idea what they mean, or which one of us is right, either way, it all links back to me.

Clearly my original plan to lie low for a while will no longer work. Not only will the crowd eventually find me, they'll go after Snelling for trying to hide me. I need to keep him out of this. I need to find another way to turn things around before it gets any worse. I need to find out why they called me the Keeper, and why they could possibly think that I'm cursed. There's only one person I can think of who might be willing and able to tell me the sort of things I need to know to restore this town to abnormal again.

I'm going to find the Seer.

Though I'm not exactly sure how or where to find the Seer or even where to start. It's not like the Seer's house can be found on a map.

But since most epic quests seem to start with a trip through the woods, I figured I might as well start mine there too.

Also, it's widely assumed that since no one actually ever sees the Seer, the Seer must live somewhere way, way out on the fringes of town. Which seems to make sense, because it's pretty much the only place where a person could hide a very strange pointy house, at the top of a very high mountain, that's riddled with all sorts of unexpected and unusual dangers. Things like carnivorous plants with long, sharp thorns that hook deep into your flesh (a rumor I'm desperately hoping has either been greatly exaggerated or is not at all true).

With no time to waste, I start trekking through the grove of crooked trees. For as long as I've been coming here, the trunks have been bent and swooped while the limbs were dramatically twisted and curved. But now, the trees are beginning to stand tall and straight like any normal grove of trees, in any ordinary place.

I quicken my pace and rush for the farthest corner I can think of—a place as far from civilization as one can possibly get and still claim a Quiver Hollows address. I make a mental list of everything I've ever heard about the Seer's existence.

This is what I have so far:

1. The Seer lives all alone in complete seclusion by choice.
2. Though no one can actually confirm the above, there has been no record of any townspeople having successfully visited the Seer. There's also no good or valid reason to doubt that it's true, since people in Quiver Hollows have no reason to lie. (People here

don't say things to make themselves appear smarter or better than anyone else.) Until a few minutes ago, this was a very content town.

3. All of which serves to support the theory that the Seer does indeed live alone, secluded from everyone else, since there's never been any real reason for anyone to ever visit the Seer. Until today, life in Quiver Hollows just flowed along nicely, with little to no effort. So with that in mind, what would be the point in making a very risky, extremely dangerous voyage through man-eating plants, just to confirm that yes, your life is right on track, and will continue to be that way forevermore?

A carpet of spongy moss dips under my feet, causing them to make slick slurping sounds as they sink and rise, rise and sink. With my flashlight bouncing along the rows of tall trees, making them appear forbidding and sinister, I try to convince myself I have nothing to fear. Not from the trees, anyway. It's people who now pose the biggest threat.

When the forest eventually yields to a clearing, I shine my light into the distance, where I'm able to just make out the shape of a long, twisted mountain that tapers to a very narrow peak. At the top of that peak, the broad, rectangular base of what I assume to be a house perches precariously, as though it might tip right off at any moment.

I creep closer and shine my light all around, unafraid of

being seen, since no one ever ventures to these parts. And I doubt they'll do so today, since they're too angry to think straight. Though I imagine by tomorrow or the next day, they'll be seeking assurances, looking wherever they can to get a glimpse of what the future might hold in such uncertain times.

Though the roofline is buried in mist, it's rumored to resemble a tall, pointy witch's hat. I guess when I make it to the top, even if the Seer does refuse to see me, at least I'll be able to confirm whether it's true.

I keep on keeping on, making my way toward the first line of defense that borders the property by way of a thick tangle of thorny vines that look impossible to penetrate. Before I can get too discouraged, I remember something else I heard. The vines are there for two reasons: to keep the timid away, and to challenge the bold to confirm just how badly they want to continue.

While I've never been timid, I'm also not very bold. I'm just a kid who needs help from the only person I can think of who might be willing to give it.

I eyeball the thorns, trying to remember if there's something more, some sort of scheme for properly breaching them.

How many late nights did we spend at someone's house trying to scare ourselves silly by swapping stories about the Seer? Lots.

How many crazy stories have I heard about the Seer over the years? Too many to count.

How many of those stories did I commit to memory? Hardly any.

I frown. There has to be a way, there has to—

And just like *that* I remember two more things:

4. The reason the Seer even exists in a place where no one ever has need of a Seer is because someday, someone will need to see him/her/it.
5. Which means the Seer has been waiting up there at the top of that mountain, for all these years. Knowing there will come a day when someone would heed the call to risk their life by breaching those vines in order to get to the truth.

Never once in my wildest slumber-party dreams did I ever imagine that person would turn out to be me.

The vines slither and hiss before me. And when I reach a tentative hand forward as a test, one of them actually shoots straight out from its stem and snaps at my nose. Since it's already swollen, throbbing with pain, and maybe even broken for all I know, the fact that the plant went right for my sore spot really gets on my nerves.

Instinctively, I leap about a foot back. While I'd like to

pretend that I'm currently fueled by a steady dose of adrenaline, purpose, and bravery, mostly, I'm not. I'm shaking all the way to my bones while engaging in the sort of dumb nonsense things I usually do when I don't really know what else to do. I straighten my tie and adjust my messenger bag so that it falls in a perfect diagonal across my chest. I am acting as though those two moves are all that's required to turn this entire situation around, when the real truth is: I don't want to do this.

Truly, on a list of things I never wanted to do, this moment right now would be number one.

But with nowhere else to go and nothing to rely on but the few tools I always lug with me, I unstrap my messenger bag and hold it like a shield while I use my other hand to swing the flashlight like a club as I plow straight ahead.

With my head ducked behind my bag/shield and my flashlight slashing wildly at the hungry, man-eating vines, I focus on putting one foot in front of the other. I cut as narrow a path as I can, repeating the phrase *"One step at a time, one breath at a time"* while steadfastly ignoring the carnivorous plants intent on eating me alive.

The vines snap and bite. They pluck my jacket straight off my back and turn my pants into a pair of ragged shorts with frayed hems. Still, I continue, driven by the knowledge that there's no use turning back, and nowhere to go if I did.

I'm so focused on fighting for my life that I've already cleared the vines by several steps before I realize I'm free. I fall to my raw and bloodied knees in relief, thankful that somehow I survived. Only, when I look ahead, I'm dismayed to see the vines have given way to something much worse than I ever could've imagined.

TEN

THE MASTER'S DISGUISE

At some point while I was busy defending my life against flesh-eating vines, I failed to notice the narrow, rickety spiral staircase crafted entirely of spikes rising dizzily before me.

I struggle to my feet and move toward it, sure it can't be as bad as it seems. But as I venture closer, I discover it's even worse than I thought.

First of all: There are no handrails.

Secondly: From where I stand, the mountain has narrowed to such a degree that one false step will see me toppling straight to my death. While at the same time, one false move on the spike-ridden stairway will result in certain impalement of my foot. In other words, there is absolutely no room for error here.

Slowly, carefully, and very deliberately, I pick my way skyward. Using only the tips of my toes for balance, I step and lift, lift and step, moving as lightly and gracefully as I possibly can. And since my true nature veers more toward lumbering and unsteady, this is no easy feat.

If there was ever a time to not be so glaringly normal, now would be it. How easy this would be if I had Ming's levitation skills—I'd flit right to the top! Or Ollie's telekinesis skills, since they would allow me to bend and dull these spikes so that they no longer posed a threat. Or even Penelope's telepathy skills, since I could put a mental call in to the Seer ahead of time to check if he was even willing to see me before I decided to risk it all on a whim.

You might think that the more obstacles I overcome, the more confidence and assuredness I'd have.

As it turns out, exactly the opposite is true.

Every step feels less like progress toward my goal, and more like progress toward my own premature death. Which leaves me questioning my plan, not to mention the sanity (or lack thereof) that had me convinced this was the only way to go.

Seriously. I could've just stuck to the original idea, which was to remain out of sight until the whole mess righted itself.

I could've even thrown myself on the mercy of the crowd and made them—I have no idea how—but made them see that I mean no harm.

But *noooo!* Instead I decided to—

Without warning, I lose my balance and teeter dangerously sideways—not unlike the strange wooden house just above that's wobbling back and forth on the tip of the peak.

A wave of panic rushes through me. My hands claw and swipe at the air, desperately seeking purchase, only to confirm that there's truly nothing there.

This is it.

This is the end.

And just like I always suspected, the experience unfolds in excruciating slow motion. So I can savor every last terrifying moment.

First I think: *What a crummy way to go.*

Followed by: *Not that anyone will ever know, since every tilt toward the abyss only confirms they'll never recover my body.*

Which then gives way to: *Funny how I've dedicated the better part of my life to memorializing dead pets only to die in such a way that no one will ever be able to memorialize me.*

I close my eyes, prepared to accept the inevitable, when I'm reminded of the lesson I learned in fourth-grade tightrope-walking class: *The key to balance is all about lowering your center of gravity.*

Immediately, I stop grasping, stop hyperventilating, stop

panicking, thrust my arms out horizontally, and bend my knees slightly. I focus on the present moment as opposed to my fears for the future and my regrets about the past. And slowly, surely, I steer myself upright again.

I balance in place for a moment, just to make sure that it really did work—that I really am stable—then, slowly, I continue climbing. Each step brings me closer to my goal, until I can just make out the tip of a long, pointy roof, which, if nothing else, proves that at least one of the rumors is true.

When I reach the final three steps, I find they've narrowed so that they're better off avoided. I set my sights on the nice wide landing at the top, hope for the best, and leap.

The soles of my shoes land solidly, thudding hard against the wide steel grate. I take a moment to get my bearings, rotate my ankles, and stretch out my calves, trying to relieve the cramps that have overtaken them. Luckily, the pain in my nose has lessened to a dull throbbing that I can easily tolerate.

Above me, the house wobbles and creaks ominously. I do my best to ignore it and turn my focus to the tall metal gate just before me.

Much like the stairs, the gate is covered in spikes of varying lengths. Some are short, some are long, but all of them are dangerously sharp, and all of them are fitted so tightly together there's no way to actually touch the gate without leaving a constellation of holes in my flesh. If that wasn't enough, there's also no latch, no handle, no way to let myself in.

I crouch down, thinking a new angle might help to uncover something I might've missed. And while it looks pretty much the same from here (albeit a little more forbidding), I notice there's something strangely familiar about . . . about the pattern.

The spikes are arranged in a pattern!

Is it a message of some kind?

A clue to how to get in?

I pace back and forth, rubbing my chin just like Snelling does when he's working out a problem, and that's when it hits me: the short spikes and the long spikes are purposely and precisely placed like pieces of a puzzle, and suddenly I know beyond a doubt that Snelling was here.

Snelling created this gate.

And maybe even that treacherous stairway.

He's the only metal bender in town with enough mastery to craft something so detailed, complex, and deviously extravagant.

A closer look proves that I'm right. The pattern I noticed is actually Snelling's symbol—a dragon wrapped around the letter *S*.

Snelling made it and signed it, and luckily for me, I'm probably the only one in Quiver Hollows (besides Snelling) who knows just how it works.

Slowly, tentatively, I press my index finger against the spike that serves as the very tip of the dragon's tongue, using just enough force to prick my skin. It releases a bubble of blood that trickles down the length of my finger and pools in my palm.

The latch springs open, the gate yawns wide, and I find myself standing on the front porch of the strangest house I've ever laid eyes on.

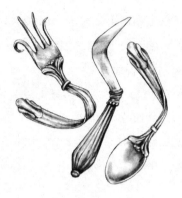

ELEVEN

NOT-SO-WELCOME MAT

At first glance, the wooden house reminds me of a fortress—an old, abandoned, weather-beaten, warped fortress with a tall pointed roof that really does resemble a witch's hat. Like most houses in Quiver Hollows, the walls are distorted. Only, these walls are even puffier and more swollen due to the concentrated shroud of mist, fog, and clouds that surround it. Though from what I can tell there's not a single window or door—no discernable way of getting in or going out.

It's like someone purposely placed a rather large wooden

box at the top of a mountain peak, slapped a roof on it, and decided to call it home.

Oh, and that awful creaking, groaning noise I've been listening to for the better part of the journey sounds even worse now that I know the cause. Every shift of wind sends the place teetering, to the brink of sliding right off the top of the mountain before it somehow miraculously rights itself again.

As far as houses go, this is the oddest one I've ever seen, and considering where I come from, that's really saying something.

While it feels like a victory just to have made it this far, I'm really in no mood for celebrating. For one thing, it's bitterly cold up here at the top of the mountain. For another, every time a breeze kicks in, the whole house starts seesawing. I'm so queasy I feel as if everything I've eaten over the course of the day has collectively agreed to make the reverse trip back out. Then, just when I'm sure I'm really, truly going to lose it, the house rights itself, my stomach stills, and the mist settles in a way that leaves everything murky and obscured.

If Quiver Hollows ran on logic (which it clearly doesn't, but if it did), you'd think that if the legend was true and the Seer has spent a lifetime waiting for me and perhaps he/she/ it would extend a little hospitality. Maybe put out a welcome mat, or at least offer me a viable way in.

I mean, just how far am I expected to go in order to prove myself?

Haven't I done enough already?

What could the Seer possibly expect of me now?

I'm so busy fuming it takes a moment before I catch a glimpse of the long, thick rope dangling from an open window about four stories up.

Figuring it's the best I can expect by way of a welcome, I grab hold and start climbing.

TWELVE

DOPPELGANGER

"Don't. Move."

They're the first spoken words I've heard since I left Snelling's house, and as luck would have it, it's the last thing I wanted to hear.

"Seriously. Not so much as an inch."

I'm balanced on the windowsill that's a lot narrower than I expected it to be, while once again, the house gets to see-sawing violently.

"Now, on the count of three," the voice says, "I want you to jump. Do not hesitate. Just trust me and do as I say."

Trust you? I haven't even seen you!

The words stay trapped in my head, while on the count of three I do as I'm told.

In an act of blind faith, I leap. My body seems to hover, defying gravity for a handful of seconds; then I crash onto the surprisingly soft cushions of a pink flowered couch. It zoomed up just in time to catch me, before shooting wildly back toward the other side of the room.

I brace myself, watching in horror as the wall rears up in front of me. I'm moments away from what could only end in a violent smashup, when the runaway sofa halts and spins around so abruptly I pitch forward. I'm nearly ejected from my seat, and then I smack back against the cushions, the whole room goes still, and from seemingly out of nowhere, the Seer presents her/him/itself.

"Now tell me, how can I help you?" a young male voice asks, but all I can do in reply is blink, stare, then blink and stare some more.

It's like looking into a fun house mirror. The boy looks exactly like me, except I'm sitting on a pink flowered couch and he's sitting on a stiff-backed chair on the opposite side of the room. Also, my suit is torn to bits, while his is clean and pressed. As I survey the space, I notice that all the furniture is on tracks, which explains the sliding, stopping, and spinning.

"I assume you're here for a reason," my look-alike barks

impatiently. This is something I would never do to someone who just experienced the level of terror that I went through.

I slide my messenger bag off my shoulder and place it on the cushion beside me. If nothing else, the act buys me a little time until I can settle on a strategy. Deciding a direct approach is best, I get right to the point. "I'm here to see the Seer."

"Congratulations!" The Seer claps his hands together in a show of false glee. "Mission accomplished!" he cries, while all around me the room rains endless amounts of confetti. "And now that you've seen me, shall I prepare the rope for your departure?"

I'm seething. I'm covered in iridescent confetti and seething.

Reading my expression, he says, "Oh dear, you look a bit . . ." He cocks his head, places his messenger bag beside him like I just did, and finishes his statement. "Mad. You look very, very mad. Which is not a good start, I suppose. Not a good start at all. So why don't we begin again by introducing ourselves? As you already know, I'm the Seer, and you are . . ." Before I can reply, he says, "No, don't tell me, I know this one! After all, it's like looking at a far more tragic version of myself!"

"Grimsly. Grimsly Summerfield," I say, starting to bolt from the couch, thinking I've had enough and am ready to cut my losses and brave the trip back, when the Seer lifts a cautionary hand.

"You really don't want to do that," he says, though it's too late to heed the warning.

Merely by shifting my weight from the couch, I've set the whole house off balance to the point that the sofa is sent careering back along its track, taking me with it, as the Seer races past the opposite way. He waves to me as he rides his straight-backed chair to the side of the room where I sat just a moment before. When we both hit the end of our tracks, our seats spin around until we're facing each other again.

"That never gets old!" The Seer throws his head back and laughs as though he's actually enjoying himself. I struggle to catch my breath, not daring to so much as move, as I gaze longingly out the same window I came from. I wonder if I could possibly survive a jump from the fourth floor, because anything, *anything* is preferable to what might happen if I stay one more second in this house of crazy.

"It won't end well." The Seer frowns, presumably reading my thoughts. "I wouldn't try it if I were you. Which I'm not, despite the startling resemblance."

That's it. I've had enough of his games. I'm either going to get what I came for or not (probably not), but the least I can do is put a stop to all this and stand up for myself. I'm tired of being the punch line to his cruel, twisted joke.

"Why do you look like me?" I ask. Actually, I don't ask, I demand. The look I give him is meant to be withering. Though, from what I can tell, it wasn't exactly received that way.

The Seer adopts a more serious expression and takes a moment to contemplate. Then, in a quiet voice, he says, "Who would you like me to look like, Grimsly?"

"Yourself. You. Whatever that may turn out to be."

"Oh, I'm not sure you're ready for that." The look he gives me is challenging.

"Try me," I say, attempting to appear confident, but mostly hoping I won't live to regret it.

And even though I brace myself for whatever may come, nothing, and I mean nothing, could've prepared me for the sight before me.

THIRTEEN

SWEET FACE

"You're a *girl?*"

For the record, I'm not proud of the question. And I'm especially not proud of the derisive tone I just took when I asked it. I have nothing against girls. Two of my best friends are girls. Still, not a single story I've heard so much as hinted that the Seer was a sweet-faced, golden-haired, green-eyed little girl wearing a blue sailor dress with a white pinafore, and a matching blue bow in her hair. I'm really not sure what to make of it.

"Not what you expected?" Her voice is sugary, syrupy, and it sets me on edge.

"What are you, eight—nine?" I ask. It's like I'm determined to get on her bad side, but I can't seem to stop myself.

"I'm ageless. Timeless. Lace and fineness." She smiles at a joke I'm not sure I get. "I've lived a very long life. Longer than most. But nine was such a good year and such a good look for me, I decided to stick with it."

"So, you haven't grown since you were *nine*?" I run the idea around in my head, trying to make sense of it.

"On the contrary, I've grown plenty. Growing has nothing to do with aging. They're two separate phenomena entirely."

I'm really not sure how to reply to that. I have no idea what she means.

"Growth happens in here, and here"—she jabs a finger toward the side of her head and then in the general vicinity of her heart—"while aging happens on the outside. I decided on my ninth birthday that I liked what I saw and there was no reason to progress any further. But inside, I'm older than you would likely believe."

"So does that mean you don't celebrate your birthday anymore?" I know it's a dumb thing to say, but I'm still trying to wrap my head around all this. It's a lot to take in.

Also, I'm weirded out by how easily she switches from

grumpy to animated. It's like her moods shift as often as this strange house she lives in.

"No. I still have them. It's just that every year I'm nine again."

Outside, a breeze kicks up, a burst of mist blows through the open window, and my couch and her chair start gliding lazily toward each other, nearly meeting in the middle of the house. When the breeze dies down, we slope back to our separate sides.

"Why don't you just put a lock on these things?" I ask, tired of all the back-and-forth, the complete unstableness of this place. "Or bolt the furniture down so everything stays put?"

She looks at me then. Even though she's clear across the room, it feels like she's sitting as close as my knees.

"Because nothing is meant to stay put. The universe is a vast and wondrous place of constant motion and change. And since I spend my whole life inside, stuck at age nine, this helps remind me of that. Also, it's fun!" She grins brightly for a moment before her lips fall flat and her gaze turns serious. "So, Grimsly Summerfield, tell me—do you have any other deep observations, insights, or questions before we begin?" She assumes the appearance of a person who is waiting patiently, even though I'm sure that couldn't be further from the truth.

I shake my head and try to quiet my body language, forcing my leg to keep from involuntarily kicking and my hands to stay folded sedately. Whatever it takes to keep her from getting annoyed and setting this house in motion again.

She nods briskly, sending her blond curls bouncing over her forehead. Then she rises from her chair and says, "You know the drill by now, so hang on tight."

Before I realize it, I'm back on the other side of the room while she stands frowning before a very tall bookshelf built into the wall that just a moment ago was right beside me.

"Oh dear." She shakes her head and taps her fingers against the skirt of her dress. "I'm afraid it's on the uppermost shelf. So high up, even you can't reach it. Even though you are rather tall for your age."

"What is? What's on the uppermost shelf?"

"Your prophecy!" she spits, rolling her eyes but stopping just short of saying *duh!* She acts as though she just said something glaringly obvious when that's hardly the case. I have no idea what's going on.

"Unfortunately, this means I'll have to wake Sir Jinxly." She bites her bottom lip and makes an exaggerated worried face. "Sir Jinxly does not like his sleep being disturbed, but then, who does, right?"

Without warning, she presses two fingers to her lips and lets out a very loud, very strange whistle. A few seconds later, an extremely fat cat with bright blue and green spotted fur emerges from a plush velvet cat condo I didn't notice until now.

"He's here!" The Seer claps excitedly as Jinxly the cat slowly approaches, dragging his considerable belly against the hardwood floor. "The one we've been waiting for has finally arrived!" she squeals. "So, up—up you go now! Up—just like I trained you!"

The cat blinks its sleepy long-lashed eyes at her but otherwise doesn't so much as budge, leaving me to wonder just how long ago this training took place. Sir Jinxly looks like he's spent the majority of his life doing little more than napping, eating, and riding his cat condo from one side of the house to the other.

"So that's the way you're playing it, huh?" The Seer plants a hand on each hip and whispers to me, "He always demands to get paid first, and I find it very vexing." She heaves a loud, dramatic sigh and marches toward my side of the room, which sends the house teetering and creaking and leaving me queasy all over again.

She returns with a handful of fish- and bird-shaped cat treats. Jinxly devours them with the sort of delicate greed that would be fascinating to see if I weren't so busy being nauseous and waiting for the seesawing to end. His snack finished, he licks his chops, his paws, and his fur and with a string of satisfied purrs settles onto a pile of confetti for a nice long nap.

"Hey—deal's a deal." The Seer towers over him, her voice so commanding the cat hisses in protest. Still, a moment later, I watch as the enormous feline crouches down low, tenses his body, and makes a glaringly reluctant yet amazingly agile leap toward the sky.

Instinctively, I cringe. I'm just not sure there's enough magic left in this world to defy the laws of physics in the way this oversized cat is determined to do. Then, surprisingly, Jinxly soars gracefully through the air before landing with a pleasantly solid thump on the topmost shelf. He noses around for a bit, upending a few old hardcover and paperback books that spill to the floor, before locating a rolled-up piece of what looks to be parchment. Then he springs back to the ground with the prize clamped between his incisors.

"Well done!" The Seer grins proudly and reaches for the parchment, but Jinxly refuses to give it up. "Fine." The Seer huffs, reaching into her pocket. "On the count of three. One . . . two . . . ." Right on three, she drops a pile of treats to the floor and Jinxly surrenders the scroll.

"I love him, don't get me wrong." The Seer shakes her head. "But he can be really exhausting the way he insists on manipulating me." She mumbles to herself and settles onto her chair as Jinxly disappears back into his cat condo. "Anyway, here." She tips forward in her seat and rolls the parchment across the floor to where it lands at my feet. "Anything and everything you'll ever want to know. It's all in there.

Maybe even a few things you didn't want to know. But my job is to be thorough, not to be kind or to spare your feelings, so keep that in mind and don't hate the messenger."

I roll the scroll between my palms, surprised by how light and insubstantial it feels. With its curling corners and yellowing edges, it seems decades older than me.

"It is older than you," she says. "Much, much older, in fact. You wouldn't believe how old."

I frown. I don't really like that she can read my mind, though I guess it does offer a certain ease and efficiency.

Without another word, I remove the red ribbon, unroll the parchment across my lap, and stare in dismay.

"There's nothing here!" I cry, hardly able to believe I've been duped. This whole outlandish show with the sliding furniture and Jinxly the improbable flying cat was just some sort of joke at my expense!

I glare at her, about to let forth a string of words I can never take back, when she beats me to the punch. "If the scroll is blank, it's because you're not yet ready to see what it contains. When you are ready, the words will appear."

"How do I know that? How can I possibly know if that's true?"

"Well, I suppose you won't know until it happens. Once it happens, you'll know, but certainly not before then. Either way, all you really need to know is that it's enchanted."

I drop my head in despair, taking in the state of my

shredded suit, all the scratched and bloodied places where I was attacked by flesh-eating plants. I can't help but wonder, what was the point of all this? Did I really come all this way just so I could hang out with some crazy old lady disguised as a nine-year-old girl who gets her jollies by being mean to desperate people like me? No wonder no one ever comes to see her. She's pretty much the worst hostess ever.

She can hear me. She can hear everything I think, but I really don't care. Fine, I made a mistake by deciding to trust her—wasn't my first mistake and it won't be the last—but that doesn't mean I need to stick around so things can get even worse.

I shake my head, brush myself off, and am about to rise from my seat and take my chances going out the same window I climbed in, when she says, "If you truly did come to learn the future, then you might want to stick around just a little bit longer."

"The future's blank." I wave the parchment furiously over my head.

"That's not the future." Her voice is quiet, authoritative, and it makes me fall silent.

"The scroll is important. Extremely important, so you might want to tuck it away in your bag to ensure you don't lose it. Just because it's no good to you now doesn't mean you won't need to rely on it later. But when you do read it, make sure you do so quickly and carefully. The information will only be revealed once, and when it disappears, it's gone forever. Think of it as a living, breathing document—ever changing, always evolving."

I take another look at the supposedly enchanted scroll. Despite what she says, it just looks like an old piece of paper. Still, I shove it into my messenger bag in the slim chance she's telling the truth.

"So where do I learn about the future?" I ask.

She laughs as though I've said something funny. "Well, right here, of course. Why else did you endure such a journey? Certainly it wasn't just so you could hang out with a crazy old lady disguised as a nine-year-old girl, now, was it?"

I shrink under her gaze. I'm about to apologize for thinking mean thoughts even though I knew she could hear them, when she steadies her focus on me. The next thing I know her eyes have rolled back in her head, and then her lids disappear, revealing two large, round screens in the place where eyeballs would normally be.

As I stare into them, the images I'm confronted with change everything I thought I knew about our world.

FOURTEEN

SUPERNORMALCY

I wake up in a room so bright it feels like someone's holding a flame to the backside of my eyelids.

I bolt upright, forgetting for a moment where I am, until the sofa reacts to the sudden movement by skating back and forth on its tracks.

Right. The Seer. But when did I fall asleep, and why did she let me when, from what we now know, I have other, more urgent places to be?

The last thing I remember seeing is an image of me

standing at the very edge of the world. And yet strangely, the part that left me the most shaken were the images of Snelling.

In one, he was standing in Summerfield Lawn and his hands were dripping with blood.

In the other, he was also standing in Summerfield Lawn, but this time he was gazing in despair at the long rows of dug-up graves, the bones that were once buried inside them now gone.

As the Keeper, it was my duty to look after those bones, to maintain them, to make sure this sort of thing never happened.

Apparently, I'm the Keeper of the Bones.

Although Snelling never told me as much, he did hint at it the day he agreed to let me turn Summerfield Lawn into a graveyard for pets. His only condition being that I promise to protect the bones at any cost.

Clearly I failed at the task, seeing as how Chauncey the pony's bones are gone.

But what Snelling failed to explain is why the bones needed to be kept.

I guess that's the conversation he meant to have later. The one he started to have when that newspaper was delivered and I ran out the back door, denying him the chance.

So that's why the town blames me, because I failed to keep the bones.

Though I'm still no closer to knowing what they meant when they claimed my family was cursed.

"Will Snelling be okay?" I catch sight of the Seer standing before the window, her young face creased with worry.

"I sure hope so," she says, her voice grave in a way I couldn't have imagined it sounding just yesterday. "But I'm afraid that's just one of your problems."

I rake a hand through my hair, swing my legs off the sofa, and wait for her to continue.

"The sun is shining, which means the protective dome is diminishing, which means the magic is lessening, which means the world you've grown to know and love will rapidly change in ways you won't even recognize—unless you can stop it."

I gulp. Oh yeah, I saw that part too. According to what the Seer revealed, Quiver Hollows is indeed in peril, and supposedly, as the Keeper, I'm the only one who can save it.

Seriously, of all the amazing people with all their amazing supernatural gifts, *I'm* the chosen one.

Me.

The only superpower I have is the power of *supernormalcy*.

"Oh, and to answer your question—I let you sleep because I figured you needed it. Also, I healed your nose while you were out. It took two cycles of nightfall, but you seem to be fine now."

I stare at her blankly.

"You had a hairline fracture. I fixed it. You're welcome."

Tentatively, I run my fingers over the bridge. Sure enough, it feels normal again, less tender and no longer swollen. In addition, the cuts and scratches I received from the flesh-eating vines have disappeared as though they never existed. But what I say is, "Two days? You let me sleep for two whole days? Are you serious?"

"You have a long road ahead of you, Grimsly. But first—you need a few things."

She pulls a stack of paper from her pocket and hands it to me. "It's called money. It's what people use in the outside world to get whatever they want or need."

I stare at the flimsy rectangular pieces of paper. They're similar in that each bears a number in every corner, and in the center there's a picture of an old white man I don't recognize.

"This is what they have in place of magic." Reading the look on my face, the Seer says, "I don't understand it any better than you do." Her narrow shoulders rise and fall. "But believe me when I say that people have dedicated their lives to collecting large piles of it. Many have even died for it."

"But ... it's just paper!" Everything she said seems so crazy.

"Power is rarely about the thing itself. It's about the value you give to it. When there's a perceived shortage of something, people tend to give it even more meaning than it deserves."

"How'd you get this?" I ask.

"Like everyone else here, I have access to whatever I need. So this morning when this appeared, I knew it was so I could give it to you. But that's not all—there's a change of clothes too."

She motions toward my bag, and I reach down to find a pair of blue jeans, a long-sleeved T-shirt, a new pair of socks and sneakers, and a navy felt hat with the letters *N* and *Y* intersecting each other.

"That stands for *New York*," she says. Then, reading the question on my face, she adds, "It's a place. Trust me, people on the outside wear things like that."

I eyeball the clothes as though I'm not entirely sure what to do with them. I haven't dressed that way in years. I'm more of a suit-and-tie kind of guy.

"I assure you, if you venture into the outside world in your usual getup, you're going to either be bullied, or mistaken for someone trying to sell insurance or religion, or both. The suit will keep you from blending in, which is exactly what you need to do if you have any hope of succeeding."

And suddenly I understand why I'm the chosen one. Of all the people in Quiver Hollows, I'm the only one who can pass for normal in the outside world. And even though it makes sense, it still feels like a bit of a letdown.

"I'm not entirely sure that's the only reason," she says. But when I press for more details, she shakes her head. "Guess you'll just have to wait and see how it all turns out."

The problem is, I'm not sure I can afford to wait and see how it all turns out. I mean, isn't that the reason I came here—to bypass all the guessing and waiting and get a head start on the future?

"I showed you everything," she says. "I assure you. What you retained and what you lost is entirely on you."

While I'd love to argue with that, there's really no point. She did show me everything, or at least, I think she did. But my future was unfolding on dueling screens, which required me to keep switching my focus back and forth. And sometimes I'd get so focused on what was happening on one, I forgot to check the other. Then it was too late and I'd missed an entire segment of something that will probably turn out to be really important. In addition, none of it was shown in chronological order. It was more a mishmash of timelines and events.

Which is why, even after everything I went through to get to this point, I still don't know much more than I did before I arrived, never mind how any of this will end. All I know for sure is that I need to find my way to the outside world so I can locate the boy with the fake lobster-claw hands and take back the bones he stole. Clearly he's the one who stole them. Why would he leave the hand in

Chauncey's grave unless he wanted me to know he's the bone thief?

What the Seer failed to tell me is how I'm supposed to get to the outside world, since no one I know has ever been there before. Also, how I'm supposed to find this bone thief when he's no longer wearing the fake lobster hands, which were his only distinguishing feature since I couldn't get a good look at his face.

In other words, I'm pretty much right back where I started. But at least I have a purpose, a direction, and I guess I'll just fill in the blanks as I go.

After a quick breakfast, I clean myself up, pick random confetti bits from my hair, and change into the fresh set of clothes that, no surprise, fit perfectly. Then, when I'm ready to leave, I stand just shy of the window and say, "Is there any way you can call off the flesh-eating plants? I can't imagine suffering through that again."

The Seer laughs. "I see no reason for you to retake a test you've already passed. But, Grimsly—"

She pauses, and I sense she's about to say something I'm not going to like.

"Be careful when relying on magic. It always comes with a price."

I have no idea what she's getting at. This whole place runs on magic, and up until now it's worked fine.

"Maybe not always here—but definitely out there." She gestures toward a place beyond the window, beyond the diminishing dome of mist, fog, and clouds. "And there's no way to know what the price will be until you've already paid."

I nod vaguely, and am just about to climb onto the ledge when I remember something I wanted to ask when I got here. "I almost forgot," I say. "How do you know Snelling? I noticed his mark on your gate."

And just like that she gets this dreamy look on her face. "I liked him," she says, her voice adopting a more mature tone I'm not sure how to translate.

"Yeah, Snelling's a great guy," I mumble, suddenly feeling really uncomfortable. "One of the best you'll ever meet."

"No," she says. "I mean, yes, that's true. But what I mean is, I *liked* him." The sigh that follows says everything her words couldn't. "Though sadly, he could never see me as anything other than a nine-year-old girl."

It's weird to think how during our time together I've felt so many things about the Seer—anger, annoyance, frustration, dread, regret, fear—but now, all I'm left with is a deep sense of sadness. I can only imagine how lonely she must get living by herself in this strange, seesawing house with only Sir Jinxly for company.

"Our choices come with consequences," she says, her voice wistful, her expression faraway, as though imagining an entirely different outcome if she didn't alter her course the way that she did. "So choose wisely, Grimsly." Her gaze lands on mine.

I grasp the rope, ready to leave, and I turn back to say, "Wait—does that mean the future's not written in stone—that it's not a sure thing?"

"I couldn't possibly know." She shrugs. "I suppose that's for you to discover. But I like to think that it's malleable, flexible, and ours to determine."

FIFTEEN

MAP QUEST

If the trip to the Seer had been as easy as the trip back ... well, I suppose everyone would make the journey and the Seer would never get a moment's rest. For all my struggles on the way up, turns out the way down offers a very different experience.

Unlike the outside of Snelling's spike-covered gate, the inside is fashioned with elaborately carved metal, its blunt and polished edges smooth and cool to the touch.

The first tentative step on the stairway flattens the nails, widens the width, and offers a handrail I wish I'd had earlier.

The formerly flesh-eating plants lose their bite and merely nudge me along as I wedge my way through them.

I'm deep into the forest, headed for the fort I share with my friends, when I spot Ming dangling upside down from a very high branch near the top of a tree.

"He's here!" She calls to Ollie and Penelope, who are sitting on the tree fort landing.

"And he looks fine!" she shouts, despite the fact that they're already waving to me and descending the ladder. "I mean, aside from the odd clothes that he's wearing. And what's up with your cap? What's the meaning of that?"

Ming swings free of the branch and hurtles toward the ground in a series of perfect front tucks.

I glance from Ming to Ollie to Penelope and back again. I was hoping they'd be here. And yet, now that they are, I find myself worried.

"How's Snelling?" I ask. "Has anyone seen him?"

The three of them exchange a troubled look.

"He's okay, right?" I search their faces, desperate for answers.

"He's fine," Ollie says, but only after hesitating in a way that's not at all reassuring.

"But . . . ?" I press, knowing there's more and needing to hear it.

"But he had to build a big wall around his house," Ming says.

I stare at her blankly. I can't even imagine such a thing. Snelling building a wall doesn't make sense. I mean, sure, he's able—just look at the entrance he built for the Seer. But Snelling was always known for keeping his door open to anyone who needed him. Heck, the only reason he built a gate between his property and Summerfield Lawn was so I could feel like I had my own space. It was never intended to keep anyone away.

"People were threatening to come after you, so he built the wall to protect you," Ollie says. "Only, once it was done and he went inside the house to look for you, he discovered you were gone, and that's when he really fell apart. He sent me a telepathic message to ask if I'd seen you. When I told him I hadn't, he assumed they'd already gotten to you when he wasn't looking."

I close my eyes in shame. This is entirely my fault. I shouldn't have been in such a hurry to flee. I should've at least taken the time to leave a note to explain.

Penelope's frightened expression transforms her face to a maze of pale angles and dark hollows, making her look even more ghostly than usual.

"Everyone's gone mad." Ming translates Penelope's thoughts. "And I have to say I agree," she adds.

"And it's all because of me." I duck my head, feeling weighed down by the truth.

"Did you make it all the way to see the Seer?" Ollie

motions in the direction just past my shoulder. "Is that where you just came from?"

"How was it?" Ming asks before I've had a chance to confirm either way. "What was she like?"

I glance between my friends. There's so much to tell and no time left to tell it. In the end I just say, "She's nothing at all like what I thought. Nothing at all like what anyone thought."

"See?" Ming turns to Ollie, wearing her *I told you so* face. "He said *she*. According to Grimsly, the Seer's a *she!*"

"Listen," I say, desperate to move on from petty arguments and back to things that really matter. "I need you to do me a favor and let Snelling know I'm okay."

"Of course," Ollie agrees. "But why can't you tell him yourself?"

"Because I'm leaving," I announce. My voice catches, giving the impression that I'm afraid, or maybe not fully committed. And while I admit to having some doubts, mostly about my ability to accomplish all that I have to, I feel the need to restate my case. This time, I speak with conviction. "I need to go away for a while."

My friends study me with quiet disbelief. Ming is the first to speak. "You're leaving?" She brushes her bangs from her eyes and blinks rapidly. "You're actually leaving Quiver Hollows?"

Penelope's face takes on an alarmed expression as her mismatched eyes search mine in question.

"I'm going outside," I say, as though it's really that easy.

"But no one ever goes outside," Ollie reminds me. "No one arrives, just like no one departs. That's the way it's always been for too many years to count!"

"Well, someone made a recent visit." I think of the boy with the lobster-claw hands. "And he has something to do with all the normal things that are happening now. And while I'm still not entirely sure how it's connected, he stole some pony bones from Summerfield Lawn and left a severed hand in their place." Then, catching Penelope's expression, I clarify, "A fake severed hand." I watch as the color returns to her cheeks.

"It's not just pony bones," Ollie says. "All the bones are gone now, or nearly all of them. The graves have all been dug up."

I frown. It confirms the picture the Seer showed me.

"But I don't get it," Ming says. "I don't get any of it. What does bone stealing have to do with all the normal things that are happening?"

"And why is everyone assuming you're to blame?" Ollie asks.

"I'm not entirely sure," I admit. "But it has something to do with me being the Keeper." I study each of them, eager to detect even the smallest hint of knowing in their gazes, but their faces are blank. "I don't really understand it, but for whatever reason, I'm responsible for keeping the bones in Quiver Hollows. And when this bone thief stole them, somehow he took our magic along with them. And I'm the only one who can get them back and restore our town to abnormal again."

"Like a superhero!" Ollie says, his voice ringing with envy.

"But how do you know the bone thief isn't still here?" Ming asks.

"He's not," I say with conviction. It's one of the few things I know for sure.

"So where is he?" Ollie asks.

"Outside. Somewhere." I pull on the brim of my hat. "I don't know exactly."

"The Seer didn't reveal that?" Ming asks.

"Hard to say. There was a lot going on, and it was hard to keep up. I may have missed that part of the program." I shake my head and dismiss the rest with a wave of my hand. I have less time to explain now than I did when this started.

"So how are you going to get there?" Ollie asks.

I adjust the strap on my messenger bag and look around. I have no idea. They're right about no one ever coming or going, and I've never seen the way out drawn on any map. For a moment, I'm overcome with despair. But then I remember the so-called enchanted scroll I've stuffed in my bag.

Figuring it's worth a try, I unearth it and show it to my friends. The four of us huddle around it, and I can't help but ask, "You guys see anything?"

Three heads shake in reply, which is just what I feared. Either the Seer is having more fun at my expense and this is just an ancient piece of parchment bearing no real significance aside from its aged appearance, or it's not willing to help me just yet. Which also doesn't exactly make sense, since the Seer swore it would reveal the things I needed to know as I needed to know them. And right now I really need to know how to find my way out of Quiver Hollows.

"Maybe you're supposed to recite some sort of chant or spell," Ollie says.

If I am, no one told me.

"Maybe you're supposed to tell it what you need!" Ming says. "Go ahead, demand that it show you the way out or else!"

"Or else what?" I look at her. "It's a piece of parchment. What could I possibly threaten it with?"

"You could burn it—or you could tear it—or you could—"

Before Ming can complete her long list of all the various ways in which to torture a piece of paper, Penelope grabs hold of my hand and presses her palm flat against mine.

"She's transmitting a picture of you pressing your palm to the paper," Ollie says.

I glance between Penelope and Ollie. Penelope nods.

"You also need to make a wish," says Ming. "And try to feel grateful inside when you do, like the wish has already been granted or something."

"Why's that important?" I ask.

"Heck if I know. I guess magic likes to be thanked. I'm just translating the picture." Ming crosses her arms over her chest. "No matter how silly it seems."

I focus on Penelope standing before me. "I'm not magically inclined," I remind her. "That's what got me here in the first place, remember?"

Penelope looks at me earnestly.

"She says you don't need to be," Ollie translates. "Not if the paper is truly enchanted like you claim."

It makes sense. But only if the scroll actually is enchanted, which I'm beginning to doubt.

Still, it's worth a try. So I press my right palm against the page and wish for a map. I even picture a map in my head. And all the while, I force myself to thank the magic, which seems a little silly, but again, I need to give this my all.

"Now what?" I ask. This whole thing is starting to feel kind of hokey, even for someone like me, who's been raised on a steady diet of it.

"Penelope says don't stop the process," Ming whispers. "At least it's better than threatening that poor piece of paper with a violent death. Hey!" She scowls at Penelope.

I sneak one eye open and peek at Ollie. Whereas Ming can be pushy and combative, and Penelope dreamy and easily distracted, Ollie is pragmatic. He's always the voice of sound advice and reason.

"Can't hurt." He shrugs.

With my friends watching, I continue to press my palm against the paper, and follow Penelope's instructions. The whole bit about wishing and visualizing reminds me a lot of Snelling's chalkboard message at the School for Spoon Bending:

TO ACHIEVE IT, YOU FIRST
HAVE TO SEE IT AND BELIEVE IT.
IMAGINATION IS KEY!

It's a message that has never once worked for me. Then again, this time, the burden is on the enchanted scroll.

I try to hold on to all the wishing and feelings of gratitude, but mostly I'm feeling anxious about the prospect of leaving this place. Since that probably won't work in my favor, I take a deep breath and reset my focus, which is when Ming shouts, "*Ohmygosh*, Grimsly—look!"

I snap my eyes open to catch the outline of a map appearing on the page, as though drawn by an invisible hand.

I scan the page quickly, watching the areas all around the lines fill in with color so vibrant it seems to take on a life of its own. Portraying so many of my favorite places— Pendulum Falls, Chilling Cove, even Snelling's twisted metal house and my very own Summerfield Lawn. I watch carefully, hardly allowing myself to so much as blink, committing everything to memory just like the Seer warned me, and it's a good thing too, because a few seconds later the map disappears as though it never was there.

"It worked!" Ollie says in a voice filled with wonder.

Penelope dips her knees into a curtsy and smirks, but only for a moment before she swaps the smirk for a smile.

"Who would've thought?" Ming says, leaving me unsure if she's referring to the fact that the plan worked, or that I created magic, or to the surprising location with the red circle around it.

Either way, I agree. Who would've thought I'd actually succeed at manifesting something?

And who would've thought that the way out of Quiver Hollows has been hiding in plain sight all along?

SIXTEEN

TILT-A-WHIRL

Without another word, I'm off. Racing through the forest while my friends rush to keep up, I wend my way through a grove of trees, down a narrow path, and into what is usually a busier area of town, only to find it virtually empty.

On any other morning, this place would be bursting with activity. Shops would be open; people would be out greeting each other. But today, the storefronts are all closed, lending the town an eerie, barren feeling.

"Everyone stayed home," Ollie says by way of explanation.

"They're too alarmed by what's happening. They figure it's safer to stay inside."

"At least until you're captured and dealt with," Ming says, and though the words may seem cruel on the surface, I appreciate the honesty. No point in pretending the situation is anything other than what it is.

I take in the larger-than-life statue of Yegor Quiver crafted entirely from bent spoons. One hand clutches his hip while the other thrusts a gnarled spoon toward the perpetual dome of fog, clouds, and mist that covers the town. The statue I once found so inspirational now takes on an entirely different, more sinister meaning.

"Penelope is transmitting a picture of three giant red question marks all in a row and I'm wondering the same thing—how can you possibly lift that?" Ming asks.

My gaze moves among them. "With a little help from my friends," I say.

According to the bright red circle that appeared on the map, this is the place that leads to the outside world. And I can't believe how many times over the years we've played here, how many times we've used this as a designated meeting place. None of us ever would've guessed that it actually serves as a portal of sorts.

"Do you think it was placed here on purpose? You know, to keep people from coming and going?" Ollie asks.

I shrug. Until now it never even occurred to me that anyone would try to leave, much less visit.

"I thought you had to be pure of heart and magically minded to gain access. I thought that was how the great Yegor Quiver himself ultimately found his way in," Ming says. "And yet, if that's true, then how did the bone thief find his way here when clearly he's up to no good, which pretty much proves his heart's not so pure?" She frowns.

"Maybe there's more to the story than we know," Ollie says. "Maybe they never told us the full truth."

I circle the statue to examine it from every angle and occasionally give it a push. But all the metal makes it so heavy it doesn't so much as budge. If it's a show of strength that's needed, I'm afraid I'm doomed.

"I could try to bend it," Ollie offers.

"And while he's bending it, I could levitate to the top and give it a couple good yanks," Ming says.

Penelope lifts her shoulders and frowns.

"I prefer not to mangle the statue," I tell them. "The town already hates me enough as it is. I don't need to vandalize their hero and prove them all right."

"So, what, then?" Ming flutters nervously around me.

I circle again, sunk in a deep contemplative silence as I review what I know. Yegor Quiver wasn't the first to discover the town, but he was the first to organize it and make it into a better, more highly functioning place. Where magic once ran untamed, he taught the people to channel it in both useful and creative ways. Because of this, the town flourished like never before, and Yegor was hailed as the town father and honored with this very statue, which was made by his first class of spoon-bending students.

A class that included Snelling!

And just like that, I know I'm on to something.

"There's a puzzle," I say, knowing without a doubt that if Snelling was involved, he must've left a signature—some sort of identifying piece. And while I guess I could go ask him directly, there's no guarantee that he wouldn't try to keep me from leaving, or worse, that the townspeople wouldn't spot me and do something terrible.

"What do you mean by 'puzzle'?" Penelope looks at the statue quizzically.

"Some kind of riddle, like a button or a lever or something that will put the whole thing in motion, or somehow make it easier to displace."

With little to go on, they start jabbing, pushing, tapping on just about every piece they can reach, in search of whatever mark Snelling might've left.

Out of frustration, I toss my head back and gaze up at the fog dome, which is rapidly diminishing. And that's when I see it.

Yegor is thrusting an extra-large spoon into the air, and

on the base of that spoon I'm able to make out the symbol of a dragon entwined around the letter *S*—the mark Snelling leaves on everything he makes. And for a moment, I can't help but wonder if Snelling somehow foresaw this day—if he purposely left these clues for me along the way.

Did the Seer repay him for making the gate by giving him a glimpse into his own future?

Before I can ponder too long, I look at Ming and say, "The spoon." She's the only one among us who even stands a chance at being able to reach it. "Can you levitate that high?"

Ming rolls her eyes and mutters under her breath, "You are not seriously asking me that."

"If you can reach the tip of the spoon, I need you to pull on it, or maybe press on it," I say. "I can't be sure. Try to move it like a lever, and let's hope it works."

Just like that, she's gone from a graceful plié to a full-blown soaring grand jeté. She leaps all the way to the top of the spoon, where she grabs hold with both hands and pulls with all her might, which isn't much, considering how tiny she is.

With her legs dangling uselessly, she looks down at us and says, "Uh, guys, not sure this is the way in."

It's disappointing, to say the least. In my head, it all made perfect sense.

"In fact . . ." Ming's face fills with alarm. "Um, I think it's starting to break!"

A terrible loud crack sounds from the base of the statue as Ming dangles helplessly. We shout for her to hang on.

She swings her legs back and forth, gaining momentum until she's able to clasp the spoon handle between her knees, buying herself a few more seconds. She cries, "If this thing goes down, I'm going with it!"

The cracking sound worsens, soon followed by a horrifying pop. And before any of us can do anything to stop it, the spoon spins backward, taking Ming with it, as the base of the statue begins to swivel and shake, leaving us all to watch as the entire statue shifts off its axis and tilts precariously on its side.

Penelope presses her hands to her cheeks as Ollie shouts, "Ming, let go!"

A moment later, Ming loosens her grip and hurtles toward the ground, where she crashes right on top of us. Then we watch in a crumpled heap as the statue of Yegor Quiver continues to tilt and whirl until it's moved several feet from its original location, leaving the mouth to the outside world gaping wide open.

SEVENTEEN

DOWN A DARKENED TUNNEL

As soon as the dust settles, we scramble to our feet and peer into the dark, gaping hole, which appears to have no end.

"You aren't serious about going down there, are you?" Ming asks. "I can't see a thing!"

I gulp. Not trusting my voice to speak, I try to nod confidently, but it doesn't really work.

Penelope glances nervously between the dark hole and me.

"I think I can just make out a handrail." Ollie kneels down for a closer look. "And maybe even some steps carved into the earth. That's a good sign, right?" His voice sounds as unsure as I feel.

Handrails and crudely carved steps . . . not exactly ideal, but certainly better than what I faced on the trip to the Seer's house.

"Okay." I straighten the brim of my hat and adjust the weight of my bag. "I guess this is where I leave you, then."

"What?" Ollie squints.

"You can't be serious," Ming says.

Penelope's gaze glints with worry.

They know me so well, they can see right through me. But Quiver Hollows is in peril, and as the Keeper, I'm the only one who can fix it.

Also, I have to admit that despite my fears of the unknown (never mind how much I'll miss Snelling and my friends), it's exciting to think that for the first time in my life I'll finally get to experience what it's like to blend in.

"At least let us come with you," Ollie says.

I look at my friends, and I mean really look at them in a way I've never looked at them before. Ming with her ballet shoes, her feathered dress, and her levitating skills. Penelope with her ghostly appearance, elfin ears, mismatched eyes, and limited way with words. And Ollie . . . well, Ollie looks normal enough to maybe even go unnoticed in the outside world, but still, I can't take them with me. I won't put them at risk.

This is my wrong to right, not theirs.

"I need you guys to stay here," I say. "I need you to keep an eye on things, and to let Snelling know that I'm safe. I won't be gone long." I pause, realizing I have no way of knowing that; still, I continue. "Before you know it, I'll be back with the bones and everything will return to abnormal again, you'll see." I try to smile brightly, but it feels false on my face, so I abandon the effort.

"But you don't even know where this leads!" Ming cries. "You have no idea what's waiting for you down there!"

"The outside world is waiting for me," I say.

"Then here." Ollie pulls a bent spoon from his pocket and hands it to me. "It has more uses than you'd think."

I'm shoving the spoon into my bag when Ming hovers before me and says, "I want you to have this." I watch as she plucks a single fluffy pink feather from her dress.

"Is this to remember you by?" I ask, not sure what to make of it. "Because I am coming back. You know that, right?"

Ming rolls her eyes. "Please, like you could ever forget me. No, silly, it's to remind you to keep yourself light, to not get bogged down with fear or negative thoughts. And, who knows, under the right circumstances, it may even help you to fly."

"Doubtful." I frown, but I tuck it into my bag, next to the bent spoon Ollie gave me.

I'm just about to make my descent into the tunnel when Penelope surprises me by taking my hands into hers.

"She wants you to close your eyes," Ming says.

I'm about to remind her that whatever image she's trying to transmit, it won't work. We've tried this before, multiple times, only to end up in failure. But the look Penelope gives me is so firm I obey.

"Now clear your mind, and allow yourself to receive," Ollie translates.

Just as I figured, nothing happens. Penelope lets go of my hands and looks at me expectantly, but I just shake my head.

"She says not to worry. She says it's in there," Ming relays. Penelope winks and taps a finger against the side of my head. "You'll know it when you know it." Ming's gaze darts between us. "You'll see it when you're ready."

I'm just about to thank Penelope for at least trying and not giving up on me, when that same groaning/creaking sound starts up, and the statue begins to shift back to its original place.

"What's happening?" Ming cries.

"The hole—it's closing up again!" Ollie says.

"But how will you get back if it's closed?" Ming frets. "How will we know when you're ready to return so we can try to move it again?"

I wish I had answers, but all I know is that the statue is

tilting and whirling back into place, and if I want to make the trip, I only have a handful of seconds to do so.

Without another word, I give them each one last look and leap into the unknown.

I catch hold of the handrail just as the base of the statue slams firmly shut, leaving me in complete and total darkness.

EIGHTEEN

BOY MEETS WORLD

Clinging to the handrail with one hand, I fumble in my bag for my flashlight. But as soon as I've found it and put it to use, I'm left wishing I hadn't.

All around me lurk dark winged creatures with glowing red eyes. I tell myself they aren't really bats, even though I know they are.

Every few steps my cheek rubs against something wispy and sticky that reminds me of a spiderweb, but that's only because it is a spiderweb.

This is the exact opposite of Sweetcraft's Candy Cave.

Not one of these creatures is edible.

Funny how I once would've sworn that the journey through the flesh-eating vines and spiked stairway made for the scariest trip I could've imagined. But that was before I ventured deep into the unknown, shrouded in dampness and darkness and things that fly, crawl, slither, and snap.

After what seems like a mile-long descent, I finally reach the bottom, which is so mushy and wet it makes me want to start climbing back up again.

But I don't.

Can't.

It's less to do with commitment and dedication to my plan and more to do with the fact that the statue of Yegor Quiver is blocking my exit.

I slog through the muck, careful to keep my flashlight centered before me. I really don't want to focus on what's clinging to the walls, and I'm definitely better off not knowing the source of the constant stream of wetness dripping from overhead.

After a while, light flares at the end of the tunnel and I quicken my pace, in a rush to trade this nightmare for . . . well, possibly another, but I continue. Though it doesn't take long before I notice that the tunnel is shrinking. The ceiling is dropping so dramatically that I'm forced at first to hunch over, then to crawl on my hands and knees. I end the journey slithering on my belly.

By the time I crawl into daylight, I'm exhausted, covered in mud, and left watery-eyed and squinting against the glare of a sun so bright that I'm forced to duck my head and shield my eyes.

I struggle to my feet and take a few moments to adjust to the light so I can get a good look around. I'm surprised to find that, on the surface, anyway, the outside world doesn't look so very different from the world I just came from.

A wide lawn stretches before me. It's mostly brown, with a few yellow and green patches, nothing like the turquoise-tinged grass at Summerfield Lawn, but it's still grass. Still familiar. Something I can name and recognize, which comes as a much bigger relief than you'd think.

There's a four-story stone-faced building in the near distance, and while its shape is blocky, sturdy, and rectangular, with not a single piece of twisted metal or any other sort of magic or whimsy, somehow the sheer ordinariness of it assures me I can do this. I can navigate my way in this strange new world. If nothing else, I've finally found a place as bland and boring as I am, so it should be a cinch to blend in. Not to mention this is my destiny.

"Freak!" A group of boys walk past me, all of them sporting the same buzzed haircut, and sneering. One even throws something at me, which turns out to be an empty can that narrowly misses my head.

I duck. Recoil in shock. Unable to make sense of what

just happened, much less why they saw fit to target me. On the surface, we're the same. I don't have scales. I don't have fish eyes, elf ears, a tail, or anything else that makes me stand out or marks me as different from them. And yet the first thing they think when they look at me is *freak*? It just doesn't make any sense.

I stare after them in confusion. Then immediately realize my mistake when they stop and yell, "Hey! Whaddya looking at, freak?"

And the next thing I know, they're coming for me—all three of them marching in a single threatening line.

I know I should run, but it's like my legs have turned to jelly and my shoes to concrete. I'm useless, clueless, standing there openmouthed. I have no idea how to handle a situation like this, much less how to go about defending myself. This sort of thing doesn't happen in Quiver Hollows. There's never been a single act of bullying or violence—at least, not until recently.

The boys surround me. Squinty-eyed and mean-faced, they mutter a string of words I don't fully comprehend, though it's not like it matters when I'm so clearly outnumbered. And even if I weren't, I wouldn't stand a chance against them. I'm a suit-wearing, rule-obeying pet funeral director—not a fighter. Though a fight is clearly what they're after.

I raise both hands before me and try to slap a friendly

grin on my face. If they notice, it doesn't seem to make the slightest bit of difference.

"Hey, Gutter Rat," one of them says. The others all laugh.

Gutter Rat? I'm not really sure what they're getting at, but clearly it's not meant as a compliment.

I start to duck my head and leave, but that only seems to enrage them in ways I can't understand.

"Hey—hey! You don't get to walk away!" One of them, a kid with metal-wrapped teeth, grabs hold of my sleeve and yanks me back toward them; another kid tugs at my hat, pulling it right off my head.

"Yeah—you're not going anywhere!" This comes from a kid with a very round face covered in red spots that are sprinkled across most of his nose, chin, forehead, and cheeks.

I don't understand why this is happening. I mean, one has metal bands on his teeth, and the other has spots on his face, and they're picking on me?

"Where do you think you're going, Gutter Rat?" The one who first called me a freak steps forward. With his brown hair, pale skin, and blue eyes, he doesn't look all that different from me, which only makes it even more confusing.

"Listen," I say. "I don't want any trouble, so—" I start to move away again, but the one holding my sleeve refuses to let go. The other one, the one who looks the most like me, closes in for the kill.

"Yeah, well, maybe we do," he says. "Maybe trouble is

exactly what we're after. And maybe Gutter Rats have no choice but to go along for the ride."

I close my eyes. Just for a moment—long enough to wish I'd never come to this place. And when I open them again I see a girl storming toward us wearing a very annoyed, extremely unhappy expression on her face.

"Look out, the Spell Spinner is here!" they laugh.

"Leave him alone!" the girl shouts, oblivious to their taunts. Her eyes are menacing, lips grim, as she elbows her way between the boys. "Go on, now! Don't act like you didn't hear me!" With a hand clutching each bony hip, she glares at them with an unspoken threat, refusing to back down until they're well on their way. Then she turns to me and says, "Looks like you just met the biggest idiots in this place. And believe me, that's really saying something."

I'm so shaken by the experience I don't trust my voice, so I find myself nodding instead. All the while thinking: *How is it possible that I finally found a place where I fit in, only to be rejected at first sight?*

And to make it even worse, I was just saved by a girl half my size.

"What the heck happened to you?" The girl eyeballs me in a way that prompts me to glance down at myself to see what she sees. I'm covered in mud and completely filthy. As filthy as a gutter rat, I guess you could say.

"Um, I just . . ." I jab a thumb vaguely behind me, knowing

there's no way I can truly explain where I've been, much less where I'm going.

"Right. None of my business. Got it." She picks at the end of her ponytail as she continues to study me. "I have a tendency toward nosiness, so feel free to ignore me when I get that way. Anyway, I'm Frankie. Frankie Husker." She thrusts a hand forward, but mine are so dirty I settle for waving instead.

"Grimsly. Grimsly Summerfield," I say.

She cocks her head to the side as her dark brown eyes narrow on mine. "Well, that's a weird name, isn't it?"

The way she just says whatever pops into her head reminds me of Ming. And thinking of Ming makes me feel homesick, even though I haven't really been gone all that long. Still, I thought things would be easier here. I thought I'd be able to go about my business without anyone taking any notice of me. So I'm more than a little taken aback to find that, within moments after arriving, I'm called out as a freak with a weird name.

Funny how the thing I've wanted for as long as I can remember—to be considered weird, unique, or abnormal in some unmistakable way—is now the thing that marks me as bully bait.

"I've never met a Grimsly before. But I do like the sound of Summerfield. It's dreamy, isn't it?" Without waiting for a reply, she cracks her knuckles and says, "Right. Anyway, I'm guessing you're new around here?"

I shrug in reply. I'm definitely new, but I'm not entirely sure where this is leading, or how she can tell just by looking.

"You have that sort of stupefied, new-kid expression." She studies me intently, and I'm not sure how to respond, so I don't. A moment later, she says, "I can show you where you'll be staying. It's not much, but at least you can change your clothes and get yourself cleaned up before classes begin."

"Classes?"

"Yeah, classes. What did you think this was?" She shakes her head and starts walking, fully expecting me to follow. "And I'm serious about getting cleaned up before we start, because trust me, Headmaster Moonsliver will not approve of your grunge look. That is what you were going for, right?"

I want to tell her I don't have a change of clothes, and that I have no idea what she means by *grunge look*. I have no idea what anything means. But then I decide the less information I supply, the better. For whatever reason, she's decided to help me. And I have to admit it really would be nice to get out of the sun and rid of the thick crust of mud smeared all over me.

"I hope you weren't too attached to that hat." She glances over her shoulder, staring toward where my tormentors stand watching in the distance.

I follow her inside, eager to remove myself from their sight.

NINETEEN

DROPOUTS AND DELINQUENTS

The sign on the front of the building, just over the door, reads MOONSLIVER ACADEMY FOR YOUNG LEADERS.

"Don't let the name fool you." Frankie frowns. "This is basically a giant detention hall."

I'm about to ask "What's a detention hall?" when she goes on to explain, "Think of it as a school for orphans, troubled youth, and other undesirables."

I look her over. She might be an orphan, but she certainly doesn't look all that troubled. Then again, what do I know? So far, I don't understand anything about the outside world.

"So, how'd you end up here?" She glances over her shoulder and waits for me to catch up.

"I, uh . . ." I hesitate, reluctant to blow my cover and risk showing how clueless I am. "I was sort of . . . I flunked out of my old school," I finally say, feeling good that I stuck to some semblance of the truth, if for no other reason than it will make things easier going forward. Lies have a way of multiplying, and once that happens they're hard to keep track of. "And then I guess I ran away from home."

"Wow." Her dark eyes grow wide. "Color me impressed. I never would've pegged you as the type."

I keep quiet, knowing better than to ask what type she's pegged me as; there's a good chance I won't like what I hear.

"And you?" I figure since she's my only friend here, I might as well try to show a little interest and learn something about her.

"Me?" She grins in a way that shows off her slightly crooked front tooth as her whole face seems to brighten. Her brown eyes flash, her dark caramel skin looks illuminated from within, and her curly black ponytail bobs in a way that seems almost animated. "I robbed a bank."

I just blink. I'm not sure what that means.

"Just kidding." She laughs. "I'm one of the orphans. And yeah, in the interest of full disclosure, I also got in some trouble at my old school for—"

"There you are."

A large block of a man towers over us, and my first thought is how weird it is that he's dressed like everyone else in this place. His khaki pants are perfectly creased, his navy blazer looks recently pressed, and though his white shirt appears impeccable at first glance, a closer look reveals that the buttons are straining at the seams, overwhelmed with the task of attempting to contain his sizable belly.

But it's his face that gets me. His complexion reminds me of a ripened tomato. His features are so flat and stern, with his minuscule nose, thin gash of a mouth, and small, squinty eyes overshadowed by a pair of thick, bushy brows, that there's not a trace of kindness. I find myself staring in wonder. I've seen a lot of things, but I've never seen a person like this.

When he speaks again, his voice is so loud it sets me on edge. "Frankie," he booms. "I think it's best if you head to class now. I can escort Grimsly from here."

My head whips between them. *How could he possibly know who I am?*

Without another word, Frankie races down the hall, but not before I catch the look of fear in her eyes. The next thing I know, the man is pressing a large hand to my shoulder and steering me toward an open doorway.

"I'm Headmaster Moonsliver," he says. "And this is my academy. I expect good behavior and full compliance from all of my students, and that includes you. So I suggest you hurry and get yourself cleaned up and changed into the uniform you'll find in your room. I'd hate to have to punish you for being late on your first day of school."

Before I can ask how he knew my name when I'm not even supposed to be here, he's turned away and shut the door in my face.

TWENTY

SEWER SWINE

I'm not at all surprised to find that the uniform Moonsliver mentioned is an exact replica of what he and everybody else in this place is wearing. But since I can't exactly stay in the clothes I arrived in, I leave them in a filthy pile in the corner of the room. Then, after getting cleaned up, I study myself in the mirror that hangs from the back of the door.

The navy blue blazer, pressed white shirt, and khaki pants make me look more like the self I'm used to seeing in my black funeral director suits, yet something about them feels wrong. And not just because the fabric is scratchy and stiff, but because the uniform has absolutely no personality. It's like its sole purpose is to make us all look the same, which is pretty much the opposite of the philosophy in Quiver Hollows, where individuality rules the day.

Since there's no good reason to stick around any longer than necessary, I sling my bag over my shoulder and make for the door. At the same time, someone works the handle from the other side, and in walks the boy with the metal-wrapped teeth.

"Hey, Gutter Rat." He looks me over and sneers. "Looks like we're roommates."

And that's when I take a better look around the room and notice there are twin beds pushed against opposite walls with two small nightstands between them.

"Better get crackin'," he says. "Moonsliver sent me to find you. He doesn't abide lateness, and trust me, Gutter Rat, you don't want to make Moonsliver mad."

Just like before, he grabs hold of my sleeve and drags me into the hall, and though I try my best to break free, the kid is freakishly strong.

"You need to stop calling me Gutter Rat," I say, after I finally manage to release myself from his grip.

"Okay," he agrees, his tone friendly enough. He stops at the end of the hall, holds a door open before me, and says, "After you, Sewer Swine."

TWENTY-ONE

THESE VAGABOND SHOES

I've only been in two schools in my life, and yet I still feel pretty confident saying that all classrooms are basically the same.

There are desks for the students and an even bigger desk at the front of the room for the teacher, and adjacent to that there's a podium for the teacher to lecture from.

Also, there's a chalkboard featuring some sort of inspiring statement. Or if not inspiring, then at least something that gives a glimpse of the class theme or the day's lesson.

Snelling always wrote stuff about dreaming and believing and creating the very things you dream and believe.

Which is pretty much the opposite of what Moonsliver has written in big bold letters:

RULES-OBEDIENCE-CONFORMITY-SAMENESS
THESE ARE THE GOALS WE STRIVE TO MEET!
MAGICAL THINKING IS FOR THE PATHETIC AND WEAK!

I take the only empty seat and sneak a look across the room at Frankie, who's sitting at the desk in the front right corner. I'm hoping she'll offer some clue as to what I've gotten myself into. I thought this was a school for delinquents, not for learning how to debunk the very thing I know for sure exists.

Moonsliver stands behind his podium and steers his focus to me. "Class," he says, "we have a new student joining us today. Why don't you stand up and introduce yourself?" He gestures impatiently at me.

Reluctantly, I push away from my desk and shoot a tentative look around the room. I'm used to speaking in front of large groups. As a pet funeral director, I do it all the time. But the groups I usually speak in front of are grieving and looking to me for words of comfort and solace. They're never hostile like this, and I'm not sure how to proceed.

I make the mistake of giving a little wave I instantly

regret, then go on to say, "I'm Grimsly Summerfield." I stand lamely before them as beads of sweat race down my cheeks and pool in the starched white collar of my shirt. My classmates snicker and sneer.

"And where are you from, Grimsly Summerfield?" Moonsliver barks. Something about the way he looks at me, the way his voice catches on the question mark at the end, makes me wonder if he already knows the answer. Perhaps this is some sort of test.

But then I realize just how improbable that is; considering what he wrote on the chalkboard, Moonsliver is clearly a man who does not believe in magic.

Also, he's too old to be mistaken for the boy with the fake lobster-claw hands.

Which pretty much rules him out as the bone thief.

And another thing: even if Headmaster Moonsliver managed to find his way to Quiver Hollows, he's not the kind who could easily go unnoticed. He's big and bombastic, with a body that resembles a large sack of bricks. Also, from what I've seen, his face is fixed in a permanent scowl. Even in a diverse place like Quiver Hollows, his anger alone would make him stand out.

The whole class is staring, waiting for an answer to what should, at least on the surface, be a simple and straightforward question. Problem is, I have no idea how to answer. I don't know the names of any other places.

My cheeks heat, the sweat persists, and Moonsliver continues to study me from beneath a complicated swoop of hair arranged to conceal his impending baldness. Just as I'm seriously considering calling for a forfeit, I suddenly remember the letters on the cap the Seer gave me—the cap those bullies stole from me. "NY," I reply. All the while hoping that it really is a place, like the Seer claimed.

Moonsliver's gaze narrows to the point where the whites of his eyes are completely overtaken by puffy, fleshy lids. "New York City?" he drawls, overenunciating each word.

I nod vaguely, sincerely hoping I haven't just totally blown my cover.

"Well, who would have thought?"

I fidget uncertainly, trying not to wither under the weight of Moonsliver's glare. He doesn't believe me. The proof is right there on his face. And yet, for whatever reason, he gives me a pass when he says, "You can be seated now, *Grimsly Summerfield from New York City.*"

Then he turns toward the chalkboard as Frankie swivels around in her seat, shooting me a look that tells me I got off even easier than I think.

TWENTY-TWO

THE MOONSLIVER MAKEOVER

For the duration of class, I search for an exit.

I stare longingly at the door, tempted to get up and leave. Just walk right out and never look back.

But when I try to put the plan into action, Moonsliver whirls on me, shouting, "Where do you think you're going?"

I fidget awkwardly. "Um, to the bathroom?" That excuse always works in Quiver Hollows, so I figure it should work here as well.

"You go to the bathroom during the bathroom break only. Now sit, listen, and don't disrupt us again."

From across the room, Frankie shoots me a look that says "Sorry" as I slowly melt back into my seat. For the next thirty minutes I watch Moonsliver stand before the chalkboard, scribbling a bunch of stuff about the importance of rules, and obeying the rules, and how chaos ensues whenever rules are ignored. Though I'm not sure what the point is, since no one here is even trying to revolt.

When the bell rings, everyone jumps from their seats and I do the same. In the mad rush for the door, I lose track of Frankie, but unfortunately, the kid who stole my hat is quick to find me.

"Hey, Gutter Rat. I hear you tried to change your name to Sewer Swine, but I'm sticking with the original." His blue eyes peer into mine. "I hope you paid attention to today's lesson, because rules are what makes this academy great."

I nod. Try to slip away. I can't afford to take the bait. I need to get out of this place before I waste another second on this kind of nonsense.

I've just eased into the hall when he races up behind and grabs hold of my sleeve.

"Not so fast, Gutter Rat." He looms over me. "You wouldn't want to miss out on the new-kid initiation, now, would you?"

From out of nowhere his friends appear and form a circle around me. And though I'm not entirely sure what's happening, I know it's not good.

"Uh, I think I need to get to my n-n-next class," I stammer, noticing how everyone has disappeared into various classrooms, leaving the hallway eerily empty.

"Not to worry," says the kid who stole my hat. "This academy is family owned. It's been passed down for generations. As it turns out, I'm pretty well connected around here. Which means I've been given the authority to write you a tardy slip."

They throw a smelly pillowcase over my head, effectively blocking my vision and making me gag on the stench. Then they proceed to drag me down the hallway with my feet lolling helplessly behind me.

I'm outnumbered, overpowered. I should probably try to scream for help, but I'm pretty sure it won't matter. From what I've seen so far, Moonsliver Academy is a hostile environment.

After what feels like forever, they stop briefly and I hear the sound of a door opening and closing. A moment later, I'm being hauled down a steep set of stairs.

I stumble, trip, struggle to break free. But this only succeeds in making them laugh even harder.

"I should probably tell you, Gutter Rat, we don't tolerate freaks around here."

Since I can't see, I don't know who said it, but I'm guessing it's the kid who stole my hat. He seems to be the leader.

"There's a strict code of conduct here, and we expect you to honor it. If you want to fit in—and I'm sure you do, everyone does—then you need to look the part. Which means that mop of hair of yours has got to go."

Wait—what?

Another door opens and closes; then an ominous buzz sounds close to my ear. They rip the pillowcase from my head and yank my bag from my shoulder. I cough. Wheeze. Gasping for air, I try to bolt for the door. But the kids with the metal teeth and red spots stop me and throw me onto a chair.

"Promise this won't hurt a bit!" The hat stealer leers as he comes at me with a pair of vibrating clippers.

I kick, squirm, fight with everything I've got, but it's no use. There's no stopping them from doing what they're determined to do.

"Better hold still," he taunts. "The Moonsliver Makeover is an art."

I close my eyes in defeat. My ears throb with the steady hum of the electric razor mowing tracks across my scalp.

Long chunks of hair float past my shoulders and pool onto the floor. When they're finally done, they spin me around and force me to look in a handheld mirror.

"See? Much better." The hat stealer slaps me hard on the back.

I struggle to keep steady, but it's impossible to hide the shock of seeing my face so exposed, my hair shorn to stubble. The worst part is, I look just like them.

"Thing is," the hat stealer says, "fitting in isn't just about having the right look, it's about having the right attitude to go with it. And that means knowing your place."

He turns to his minions for backup, and they're quick to chime in with "Yeah!" and "That's right, tell him!"

Satisfied, the hat stealer grins. "Judging by your pathetic attempt to escape the initiation, you clearly don't understand who's in charge around here." He pushes his face close to mine. "Do you?"

I hold my own. I don't so much as flinch. Though it doesn't seem to make the slightest bit of difference.

"So, with that in mind," he continues, "we figured you could use a lesson in deep contemplation."

I glance at his friends, then back at him. That does not sound promising.

"We're going to allow you some alone time. Give you a chance to figure out a better strategy for surviving your tenure here at Moonsliver Academy."

For the first time since I arrived, I look around the room. There's a bare mattress on the floor in one corner and a bucket in the other. None of which bodes well for me.

"In fact, I'll even leave you this mirror. You can use it to remind yourself how much you've already changed and how far you still have to go."

The hat stealer tries to hand it to me, but when I refuse to accept it, he tosses it onto the stained and filthy mattress.

"Now, don't do anything stupid and try to hurt yourself with that." He nods toward the mirror as his mouth curves into a sinister smirk. "It wouldn't be the first time it happened, but it never ends well."

I swallow hard. Turn a worried eye toward the corner. *So the stains on the mattress are bloodstains. Good to know.*

He turns to his friends and says, "Let's see what he's hiding in that purse he carries around. Five bucks says there's lipstick!"

"Six bucks says it's *pink* lipstick!" The one with red spots laughs as Metal Teeth begins plowing through my belongings.

"I have money!" I tell them, remembering what the Seer told me about money being an object of power in the outside world. "You can have it. All of it. Just as long as you let me go."

Metal Teeth finds the strange stack of papers and starts to wave them over his head. His grin turns to a scowl when the hat stealer snatches it right out of his hand and shoves it into his pocket.

Well, that didn't go at all how I expected.

"What else?" the hat stealer asks, showing renewed interest in the contents of my bag.

"Just a bunch of junk." Metal Teeth holds up the No Fishing sign Albie gave me as proof.

They all start to laugh and I seize the moment by leaping

from my seat and bolting for the door. I'm fully prepared to forfeit my bag and the rest of my belongings if it means getting out of here.

My legs spin.

My shoes glide across the dirty tiled floor.

I can't recall a single time in my life when I've moved faster.

I reach for the door handle, my fingers twisting, pulling it open.

I'm a mere step from freedom when one hand grips my shoulder, a foot kicks me hard in the crook of my knee, and another hand punches my chest. And just like that, I'm falling backward through space.

The last image I see before the door slams shut is three mocking grimaces.

TWENTY-THREE

THE SKELETON CREW

I have no idea how long it's been since they locked me in this room.

There are no windows. And the only door is sealed so tightly not a single ray of light can creep in.

All I know is that it feels like an eternity. And the worst part is, I get the distinct feeling that not every student they forced in here made it out alive.

It's not like I can see ghosts or communicate with the dead. Though I know people in Quiver Hollows who can. I'm mostly going by the energy of the place. The way the atmosphere hangs heavy with the lingering fragments of unyielding despair.

Or maybe that's just me.

Although I try to stay positive, keep my hopes up, and trust that someone will come for me eventually, each passing minute makes it harder to imagine.

The Seer never showed me this part of my future. And if she did, I must've missed it. In fact, I can't recall a single thing that's going to happen at this academy. Which means I'm forced to wing it.

After what feels like hours of pacing, I find a space on the floor far from the mattress and bucket and settle in.

I've cycled through endless hours of fitful sleep and extreme discomfort when the door slams open, and a man wearing the same uniform and the same buzz cut as me shouts, "On your feet! Now!"

I struggle to stand. Wobbling unsteadily, I reach for the wall in order to right myself again. Seems like days since I last had anything to eat or drink, and it's left me lightheaded, weak, and painfully thirsty.

He throws my bag at me, and I instinctively wrap my arms around it when it nails me right in the chest. A quick peek inside assures me all my belongings are intact. Except the money, of course.

"Follow me!" he barks, leading me to the cafeteria, where he orders me to eat, then promptly leaves.

Not knowing what else to do, and overcome with hunger and thirst, I grab a tray and join the line. But when I see the disgusting array of beige lumps they dump onto my plate, I'm pretty sure I'll remain hungry until I can make my escape.

I claim a seat at the only empty table in the place. And after guzzling three large cups of water, I force myself to eat. With each bite I remind myself that I need to regain my strength if I'm ever going to find a way out of here. It's the only way I can gag down the food.

"So you made it."

I look up to see Frankie sliding onto the bench opposite me. She pushes her glass of water toward me.

"I wasn't sure you would." She studies me closely. "It's been three days since I met you."

I stare dumbstruck. *Three days?*

"You're one of the lucky ones. Not everyone makes it out of the cell."

"The cell?"

"The room with the bucket and the disgusting bloody mattress?" Her gaze moves over mine. "That's where you were, right?"

I drum my fingers on the table and sigh.

"You can go a while without food, but I'm pretty sure you can only last a week without water. Now drink." She motions toward the cup she placed before me.

"Why didn't you warn me?" I drain the water, regretting

the way the words sounded so angry. Still, they're out there now and there's no taking them back.

"It wouldn't have made a difference." She shrugs. "Everyone gets the Moonsliver Makeover and Attitude Adjustment, including the girls. Though they let us grow our hair back as long as we keep it secured in a ponytail or a braid."

"What's the point?" I ask.

"To keep you in your place. To show you who's in charge. To erase any and all lingering traces of individuality. Tell me, did it work?"

I clench my jaw and stare at my miserable tray.

"You're not really from New York City, are you?" Frankie rests her elbows on the cheap fiberglass table with her fork poised in midair and stares at me with narrowed brown eyes, as though daring me to lie.

All around us the food hall pulses with activity. Though luckily, my classmates have decided to ignore me. Everyone but Frankie.

"Well?" It's clear she won't let me off easy.

I shake my head. "Never been."

"So why'd you lie?"

I shrug. There's no good way to explain, so I don't even try.

"Does it have something to do with running away?"

I swallow hard and mumble, "Yeah, sure," figuring it's as good an excuse as any, and not so far from the truth. Then I watch in silence as she picks at the food on her tray, the tines of her fork poking into twin piles of lumpy beige mush that tastes as bad as it looks.

I can't stay here. Every moment in this place is a moment wasted. I just need to find the right time to slip away when no one is watching. At the moment, Frankie is the only one watching, but it's enough to keep me rooted right where I am. I need to come up with a plan and maybe even try to consult my enchanted scroll again.

"Tell me, are you always this twitchy?" Frankie drops her fork onto her plate and pushes the tray to the side.

I squint. I have no idea what she's getting at.

"The way your eyes are always darting around, it's like you're either plotting a heist or planning to run away again. Neither of which will end well in a place like this. There's no way to escape."

Our eyes meet.

"Seriously. No one leaves. Not ever. Or at least not without Moonsliver's consent, and even then, since no one ever hears from the person again, there's no way of knowing what really happened to them." She shakes her head ominously. "This is a life sentence, Grimsly. Most of the faculty started as Moonsliver's students. I guess after a while, they get inside your head so deep it becomes a way of life. Or maybe that's not it at all. Maybe it's just after years of failed rebellion, some people decide it's easier to give in and become what Moonsliver wants."

"And you?" I ask, suddenly overcome with worry for what might happen to her if I leave her behind in this horrible place. Yet I can't exactly take her with me—can I?

She grins. "Me? You don't have to worry about me. I may be small, but I know how to fight and stick up for myself. They won't wear me down, no matter how hard they try."

Her words are delivered with such a ferocious punch I can't help but believe her. But when she falls back into silence, when her spine caves and her shoulders hunch forward, I'm worried all over again.

"Surely there's a way out," I say. "Surely—" Before I can finish, Frankie is shaking her head.

"I'm assuming you saw the big gate out front? The one with the giant lock?"

I pretend I did, since it's not like I can confide that I actually dragged myself on my belly through a tunnel to get here.

"Well, the moment it clicked shut behind you, that was it. Your fate was sealed."

The words are just beginning to settle around me when she says, "Unless, of course, you didn't enter through the gate?"

Something about the way she looks at me makes me wonder if she knows the truth. But just like with Moonsliver, I'm quick to dismiss it, telling myself that's not possible. Because it isn't—is it?

"I mean, you were all covered in mud." Her gaze grows increasingly skeptical as I look around. Luckily, I'm saved by the bell.

"What happens now?" I ask, eager to change the subject to something that might actually help me find my way out.

She glances around the food hall, watching as our classmates begin pushing away from their tables and clearing their plates. "Mandatory study hall." She gets to her feet and picks up her tray as I do the same.

"And then?" I follow her to the place marked TRAY DEPOSITORY.

"After that it's lights-out. Then tomorrow, we get to rise with the sun and repeat the whole glorious sequence all over again. Same schedule, different day. Sometime soon they'll give you your work assignment. Since you're new, you'll probably get bathroom duty. Which means you get to clean all the toilets with a jug of bleach and a toothbrush, until the next new kid comes along and you get promoted to trash collector or something equally glamorous. Welcome to the rest of your life, Grimsly Summerfield."

The way she says it, her voice and expression so bleak, I can't help but ask, "How long have you been here, Frankie?"

"Too long to remember." She sighs, but somehow I doubt that it's true. I'm willing to bet she's been keeping track down to the exact hour and minute of her arrival.

"Do you ever dream of leaving?" I ask.

The look she gives me is so determined it takes me aback. "Every second of every day."

After weighing the thought, against my better judgment I say, "And what if I told you there actually is a way out?"

Frankie sighs. I reach over her shoulder and prop the door open as we both head outside. "Then I'd say you're as delusional as every other kid on his first day in this place. But don't worry, it won't be long before they break you too."

I ponder her words. "They didn't break you."

She shakes her head. "And they never will."

"Well, they won't break me either. You'll see."

The look she gives me tells me that while she might want to believe me, she's heard it all before, only to be left disappointed.

Another bell rings. "That's the final call to study hall," she explains.

"And what would happen if we were to skip study hall?"

"Not possible." She folds her arms across her chest. "No one skips study hall."

"But what if we did?"

She shakes her head and dismisses the thought with a wave of her hand. "Forget it. Seriously. They'll find you, Grimsly. There's nowhere to hide. And if there were, believe me, I would've found it by now."

"I thought you said they'll never break you?"

"They won't!"

"Sounds pretty broken to me."

She screws up her face. "You have no idea what you're getting into, no idea what you're starting." She plants herself on the lawn right in front of me. "I'm just trying to warn you and be a good friend. Because from what I can see, you don't really have one."

She's right about that. Still, I didn't come here to make friends. I came to find the bone thief and . . .

She walks away, heading toward the building with the sign reading STUDY HALL.

"Hey, Frankie," I call.

She spins on the tips of her toes, once again reminding me of Ming.

"What's that?" I point across the field toward a group of kids dressed in white jumpsuits, wheeling large piles of something that appears to be quite heavy, judging by the way they struggle to push it.

"Skeleton Crew," she says. "And trust me, you don't want any part of that."

TWENTY-FOUR

INSIDE VOICE

I watch Frankie disappear inside the study hall, and after a moment, I follow. For one thing, I want to hear more about the Skeleton Crew. For another, she's right about skipping study hall—I don't know the rules well enough to break them just yet.

I shadow her to a long wooden table at the far end of the room and take the seat across from hers. She pulls a book out of her bag and I do the same. After a few minutes of pretending to read, I look at her and say, "What exactly is the Skeleton Crew?"

She frowns. Her gaze darts furtively as she whispers out of the side of her mouth, "Not here, not now. There are eyes and ears everywhere." Then she makes a point of ignoring me while I look around, trying to determine just what she might mean by that.

In Quiver Hollows, the library was purposely made to look as old and grand as the books displayed on its shelves. One of my favorite things is to spend an entire day poring over the magical volumes with illustrations that come to life with every flip of a page, where the characters can actually speak for themselves. And also where, if you're really into a particular story, you can carry your book into a designated room that allows you to immerse yourself in that world. Or even create a completely different ending for a story if you're not happy with the one the author gave you.

Needless to say, the Moonsliver Academy library/study hall is nothing like that.

Where Quiver Hollows is a colorful, vibrant, lively, imaginative place, this building is dull and bleak, consisting of varying shades of brown brick and gray concrete, its shelves filled with bloated, boring old tomes, their dull, dehydrated pages offering the sort of stories you never wanted to know.

Everyone around me seems to be studying dutifully, or at least putting on a good show of it, including Frankie. She scribbles furiously with her pencil, filling an entire page of her notebook.

I lean toward her, wondering what she could possibly find so fascinating that she sees fit to take notes, when I discover she's not taking notes at all. She's writing a note meant for me.

The SKELETON CREW =
A group of kids—mainly boys—handpicked by
Moonsliver to _____?????????????????????
??
??
??
??
?????????????????????
While nobody really knows what they do, it's widely
believed that they're dangerous and scary and that
it's best to stay out of their business in the hopes
that they'll stay out of yours.
UNDERSTAND?

When she writes that last part, she looks directly at me. I nod as if I do indeed understand and I'll do my best to stay out of their way, but now that I know what I know, there's no way I can do that.

From what I've seen so far, the main goal of this place is to kill imagination, crush all creative impulse, and bully people into believing that they live in a magic-free zone.

But I was born in a place where it's understood from a very young age that everything—and I do mean *everything*—is connected in some meaningful way.

There's no such thing as coincidence.

Synchronicity is a very real phenomenon that should never be ignored.

And so, when I'm out looking for a bone thief and I come across a thing called the Skeleton Crew, it's clearly no accident that I wound up here.

The tunnel led me to the exact place I most need to be.

TWENTY-FIVE

MIDNIGHT RUN

Just after lights-out, I crawl into bed, settle under the covers, and stare wide-eyed at the water-damaged ceiling as I wait for my roommate to fall asleep.

Since it's my first night in this bed, I have no idea what to expect or how long it might take. But I guess a long day of bullying and acting like a jerk must have left him exhausted, because it's not long before he begins snoring, which I take as my cue to leave.

I sling my bag over my shoulder and exit. Shutting the door quietly behind me, I tiptoe through the hall, creep down the stairs, and am just making for the set of large double doors when someone steps from the shadows and says, "Wow, you don't scare very easily, do you?"

Frankie.

I instantly recognize her voice. But that doesn't mean I don't react by jumping nearly twenty feet into the air.

"On second thought, maybe you do." She laughs softly—loud enough for me to hear but not to wake anyone in the vicinity. "And yet that doesn't seem to stop you," she says, once I'm recovered and on the move again. "Seriously, I wouldn't touch that if I were you," she warns, just as my hand is about to make contact with the door. "It's alarmed. And seeing as how you're wearing socks and walking on the tips of your toes, I'm guessing that means you're not exactly looking to be caught."

"So how do we get out of here?" I turn to face her, startled to find she's inched so close she's just an arm's length away.

She puts her hands on her hips and rocks back on her heels, letting me know she's in charge around here.

"Depends," she says. "Where is it you're looking to go?"

Without hesitation I say, "I want to find the Skeleton Crew."

"Pretty sure I warned you against that."

I frown. She frowns. Clearly we've reached an impasse.

Somewhere nearby, a door creaks on its hinges, the sound echoing loudly through the mostly empty hall. Whether it's a door opening or a door closing, there's no way to be sure, though I certainly don't want to stick around long enough to find out.

Frankie grabs my arm and drags me down the hall and through the first unlocked door we find. Going by the scent of cleaning fluids and bleach, I'm guessing we've entered a janitorial closet.

"Shhh!" she warns, as though I don't know that when hiding in a closet it's best to stay shushed.

The two of us watch through the narrow crack between the door and the jamb, spying as Moonsliver, along with a group of boys, two of whom I recognize as the bullies who have continued to terrorize me, breeze past our hiding place before heading down a long hall, where they then disappear out the door and into the night.

"Where are they going?" I ask once the door has closed behind them.

Frankie steps into the hall, where the slant of security bulbs casts a host of spooky shadows on her face. "My guess would be the lab."

"At ..." I want to quote the time, but I'm not wearing a watch, so instead I say, "At this hour?"

Frankie quirks a brow. "Only one way to find out." She takes off in the direction they headed as I slip my feet into my shoes and race to catch up.

TWENTY-SIX

BONE DUST

"Why are you helping me?" It's a question that has to be asked. But whether Frankie will choose to answer is anyone's guess. I watch as she pauses just short of the door Moonsliver and the Skeleton Crew exited through. "Why are you putting yourself at risk?"

"Maybe I'm bored." She shrugs as she exits the building. "Maybe I'm just messing with the new kid." She glances over her shoulder and shoots me a look I can't read. "Impossible to know for sure. Though I guess you'll find out eventually."

We walk in silence, our feet cutting across the wet grass, leaving the blades underneath soggy and flat.

"You're not the only one with questions, you know." She stops in the middle of the lawn and turns on me, which seems like the absolutely wrong thing to do if you're intent on not being seen.

Which then leads me to wonder: Is Frankie setting me up? Is she only pretending to be nice?

"What do you want with the Skeleton Crew?" Her dark eyes roam the length of my body, settling on my bag for a few moments, before she lifts her gaze to meet mine. "What exactly is it you're looking for? And what's in that bag you insist on lugging around?"

I shake my head. I have no idea whether I can trust her, but this—the way she interrogates me—has me thinking I can't.

"Just as I thought." She nods as though she's not the least bit surprised. Though to be honest, I have no idea what she's getting at until she says, "You don't trust me."

I stare at her, speechless. She's offended that I don't trust her? After everything she just said that pretty much proved I shouldn't?

After a long, tense moment, she's on the move. "Then again, you can't really trust anyone here." She quickens her stride.

"Where are we going?" I ask. "Where are you taking me?"

I'm no longer sure I should follow. It's entirely possible she's leading me straight into a trap.

"To the lab," she calls over her shoulder as she hurries across the lawn.

"What's the lab?" I ask.

She stops just outside a building and says, "Someday you'll have to tell me all about the weird place you come from that we've already determined is *not* New York and apparently doesn't have a lab. But for now, let's just say it's a place where you conduct experiments and learn how to build stuff."

"What kind of stuff?"

"Stuff." Her slim shoulders rise and fall. "Heck if I know—girls aren't allowed inside. They make us take classes in cooking, cleaning, and sewing instead."

"Sounds awful," I say.

"It can be." She sighs. "Anyway, why don't you see for yourself?"

She gestures toward the building that differs from the others in that it has two large wooden doors in front and no windows, from what I can tell. Luckily, both doors have been left wide open, which would allow us to get a good look inside if we weren't forced to stick to the shadows and squint across the distance to avoid getting caught.

From what I can make out, the room is large, with high ceilings, lit by rows of naked lightbulbs that hang from the overhead rafters. There are several wide tables piled high with what look to be tools and other assorted items that I can't really distinguish. Over in one of the corners sits a large, heavy-looking piece of machinery—like a big metal box with a spout sticking out its side. A small group of kids are hovering around it.

I watch as a kid in a white jumpsuit struggles to push a wheelbarrow piled high with something I can't quite make out toward the machine. He stops near it and, along with a few other Skeleton Crew members, begins emptying the contents of the wheelbarrow by handing each individual piece to the kid standing on a platform. The kid then dumps the piece into the machine, which grinds and crushes it to a finely milled dust. The dust then pours through the spout and into a large barrel placed just beneath it.

I continue watching, creeping the slightest bit closer when I see how they struggle to lift a particularly large heavy piece that looks . . .

That looks just like a rib cage—*a rib cage the size of a small pony's!*

Could it be Chauncey's?

"What on earth are they doing?" I say, not realizing I've spoken out loud until I hear my own voice echo around me. I turn toward Frankie, only to find Moonsliver has taken her place.

TWENTY-SEVEN

WISHING PAPER

The moonlight cuts across Moonsliver's leering face, leaving half of it masked in darkness and the other half highlighted in the most grotesque way. He looks even more sinister than he did during the day.

Frankie cowers behind him, her eyes wide with fright. And even though I should probably be scared, I'm too stunned to feel much of anything.

In a sense, I guess I got what I came for. I found the bones. And while I'm sure Moonsliver isn't the boy with the fake lobster-claw hands, there's no doubt he's somehow connected to him.

And yet, I'm still left with so many unanswered questions, like:

What exactly is Moonsliver doing with the bones?

Why is he grinding them to dust?

What could he possibly be using them for?

Of course, it's not like I'm about to ask him for the answers.

"This does not bode well on your first week here." Moonsliver glowers. "And to think I had such high hopes for you." The mocking laugh that follows tells me that none of what he said is even remotely true. "Only goes to prove you can change the hair, but sometimes adjusting the attitude takes a bit longer."

I turn away and peer toward the double doors where the boys continue to feed the machine. The constant dull grinding hums steadily as great puffs of bone dust rise and spin, clumping briefly into small clouds before falling and settling back into the barrel.

"Come with me, Grimsly."

I dig my heels into a dead patch of lawn and stay rooted in place.

"This is not an RSVP situation," he says. "There's no declining this particular invitation."

Moonsliver grabs me by the collar and, along with Frankie, drags me toward an ominous-looking building. It's a shack made entirely of metal, from what I can tell.

He rips the bag from my shoulder and shoves us inside. "What do we have here?" he taunts, blocking the doorway as he leisurely sifts through my belongings. And I can't help but wonder if he'll find any more meaning in them than my bullies did. "Well, I can tell you right now that you certainly won't be holding on to this."

He waves my flashlight before me, flips the switch, and angles it under his chin so the beam of light highlights the paunchy folds under his eyes as he pulls his lips wide. Roaring with laughter, he tosses the flashlight over his shoulder, where it lands with a barely audible thud on a patch of dead lawn just behind him.

"And this?" The creases around his eyes deepen as he unrolls the enchanted scroll and inspects it from both sides. I fight to keep myself calm, my face impassive. I can't afford to do anything that might alert him to the paper's importance.

He holds my gaze for a handful of agonizing seconds before he crumples the scroll and tosses it over my head, where it lands in a far corner of the room. Next, he goes straight for the pink feather that Ming plucked from her dress and gave to me just before I set off on this ill-fated journey. After waving it under his nose a few times, he drops it to the ground and it lands next to his feet.

When he finds the bent spoon Ollie gave me, Moonsliver's face becomes so enraged he can barely contain it. "This!" He thrusts the spoon toward me, pressing it so hard against the tip of my nose I can only hope he doesn't fracture it again. Especially after the Seer was kind enough to heal it. "Why am I not surprised?" He yanks the spoon away and holds it before him, studying it with a look of contempt. "I hate to break it to you, but this sort of thing is not allowed here!"

His nostrils flare. His lips flatten and thin to the point where they look more like a wound and less like a mouth. His reaction is so overblown, so out of context, I have no idea what to make of it.

And what exactly did he mean when he said "This sort of thing is not allowed here"?

He couldn't be referring to the spoon itself. They have spoons in the food hall.

So did he mean the fact that the spoon was bent by magic?

And if so, how did he know it was bent by magic?

In the outside world, wouldn't it be more reasonable to assume that the spoon somehow just ended up bent through no mystical means whatsoever?

I'm so lost in thought that I almost miss it when Moonsliver hurls the spoon behind him, where it zings against the flashlight and lands with a quiet thump on the lawn. After he's inspected the contents, Moonsliver grunts inexplicably and shoves the bag into my chest so hard I stumble backward and inadvertently crash into Frankie. Then the two of us watch in stunned silence as the metal door clangs shut and the outside lock clicks firmly into place.

"Where are we?" I strain to see. The space is so black I can't even make out the shape of my own hand held up before me.

"We're in the hole," Frankie says.

"Doesn't really feel like a hole."

"Not a literal hole." Frankie huffs a frustrated breath. "It's just what they call it. It's weird how you always need everything explained."

Well, there it is—another weird thing about me. They seem to be multiplying.

"Anyway," she continues, her voice sounding closer this time. "If you thought the cell was bad, this is much worse. The hole is where they send the very worst cases. Whenever Moonsliver thinks you need to learn a lesson, usually a lesson in obedience, he locks you in here for an indeterminate amount of time until he figures you're ready to be a team player again."

"Does it work?" I ask.

"Pretty much always." She sighs. "Then again, going without food or water for days on end, along with other assorted means of intense deprivation and torture, usually has a way of breaking a person."

"How long do you think he'll keep us here?" I ask. Funny how I've been here four days and this is the second time I've been imprisoned.

"No idea. It's entirely possible he'll forget all about us and never return. What I do know is that we wouldn't be the first to be dragged away and never seen again. If there's one thing Moonsliver hates, it's those who refuse to conform, abide by his rules, fall in line, and/or act, dress, and think the way he wants them to."

"But what about the parents and guardians?" I say. "Doesn't anyone ever check up on their kids?"

"There are no parents or guardians." Frankie sighs. "No one cares about any of us. Everyone here has been forgotten by the world."

Where I come from, that kind of statement is impossible to imagine. After a while I say, "Moonsliver sounds like a tyrant. Why doesn't anyone ever try to revolt? Why do they all go along with him?"

"Because they're too afraid not to."

We settle in for a while, each of us lost in the landscape of our thoughts, until Frankie breaks the silence. "Tell me about where you come from."

I hesitate, not sure it's safe to confide. Maybe getting thrown into the hole is part of a deal she's made with

Moonsliver in an attempt to get me to confess everything I know about Quiver Hollows. Then again, maybe the general sense of paranoia in this place is making me paranoid too. Besides, what would be the point of all that? Moonsliver has the bones—he's connected to the boy with the fake lobster-claw hands—so clearly he already knows about Quiver Hollows. It's not as though it's a secret where he's concerned.

"It's nothing like this place," I finally say. I'm grateful for the dark so Frankie can't see the way my face threatens to crumble, the way my bottom lip trembles when I think about home and how much I miss it. Or at least the way I remember home, before everything changed.

"In what way is it different? Describe it for me." When I hesitate, she says, "Unless you can think of a better way to pass the time."

The thing is, I don't want to pass the time. I want to escape. But since Moonsliver stole my flashlight, I can't even begin to look for a way.

Still, that doesn't stop me from scrambling to my feet and running my hands all along the smooth metal walls until I reach what I assume is the door. But it's just another thick piece of metal with no inside latch or handle, no discernable way to exit.

I kick it. Slam my foot hard against it. The result being a sore toe and a door that doesn't so much as budge.

Deep inside, I can feel my pulse quickening, my nerves

starting to thrum, as a wave of panic crests from within. It's a feeling I now recognize as fear.

The first time I felt it, really, truly felt it, was on the journey to the Seer. Until then, I never had a reason to fear anything. Sure, my friends and I would all try to scare ourselves silly with late-night tales, or by reading scary books, but that was nothing like this—not even close.

No, real fear is when you're left feeling lost and alone, cloaked by dread and jangling bones. It's so miserable I'm willing to do anything to shake it. Including answering Frankie's incessant questions.

"What about your friends?" Frankie says. "Do you have any friends there?"

I force my breathing to slow. My pulse begins to settle, and slowly, I sink to the floor and sit with my back against a cold metal wall I can't even see.

"Yeah," I finally say. "I have good friends. Great friends. The best sort of friends you could ever imagine."

"What are their names?" Frankie's tone grows softer, smaller, sounding less like an inquisitor and more like someone who's truly interested in a world outside this place.

"Well, there's Ming—you actually remind me of her."

"Really?" Frankie perks up. "In what way?"

"Well . . ." I try to think of the best way to phrase it so she won't take offense. "Ming says whatever's on her mind, usually without trying it out first in her head. Which means sometimes she can seem a little harsh, but she's actually intensely loyal, and true, and she has a really good heart."

Frankie laughs in a way that sounds like equal parts pride and embarrassment, which helps me to loosen up a bit.

"Then there's Penelope—"

"Are all your friends girls?" Frankie's voice rises in such a way that, even though the room is pitch-black, I can imagine the surprised look on her face.

"No, there's also Ollie."

"What's he like?"

"Ollie's the best spoon bender around."

"Spoon bender?"

I can't believe I just said that, but now that it's out there I have no choice but to claim it. "Yeah," I tell her. "He can bend metal—and lots of other things too—using only the power of his mind. If he were here . . ." I swallow hard, needing a moment to continue. "If he were here, he could blow right through these walls," I say, thinking how ironic it is that I'm trapped in a metal room not long after failing my spoon-bending exam. As if I needed yet another example of just how incapable I am.

Frankie lets out a low whistle. "Wow. You know, I've tried that before—lots of times, actually—but I could never quite manage it. Never got so much as a dent."

After a moment, I admit, "Me neither."

"And Ming and Penelope—can they bend spoons too?"

"Sure," I say. "Everyone in Quiver Hollows can."

"Everyone but you," Frankie says.

I sigh in reply. Letting my silence speak for me.

"Why do you think that is?"

I shrug. But then remembering how she can't see me, I say, "No idea."

We sit quietly for a while before Frankie says, "Grimsly, I'm sorry about—about us ending up here."

I don't know how to respond. What's done is done. There's no going back, no stopping what's already started.

"Can I ask you a question?" she says.

"You've already asked quite a few."

She continues. "Why did you look so scared when Moonsliver pulled that blank piece of paper out of your bag? Also, what's up with the bent spoon and feather—are they mementos of some sort?"

I sag against the wall, wondering if I've shared too much already. Then, deciding to trust her with the rest of it, I go on to say, "The paper is enchanted."

"Enchanted?"

"Meaning it's magical, charmed, imbued with special powers."

"I know what 'enchanted' means," she snaps.

And then I remember something—something I heard not long after I got here. "Why did those kids call you the Spell Spinner?" I ask.

In the dark, she laughs softly. "That's just one of many nicknames. I'm also called Witch, and *Bruja* too, which is Spanish for 'witch.' Anyway, I guess it's because I have a fascination with magic. That's why I got kicked out of my old school. On my first day here, when they tried to bully me, much like they tried to bully you, I cast a spell on them."

"What kind of spell?"

"I mumbled a bunch of nonsense words that sounded like Latin and told them I woke an evil spirit from the dead and ordered it to haunt them."

"Did it work?"

"I made it work." She laughs. "I found a dead rat and hid it in one of their rooms. Told them it was the scent of the undead. And at night, I'd sneak down to the boys' dorm and bang on their walls and make scary sounds. After about a week, they begged me to make it stop, so I did. And they've mostly left me alone ever since."

"They still call you Spell Spinner," I say.

"I don't mind. I figure I earned that title, so I wear it with pride. Anyway, can I see it?" she asks. "The enchanted paper?"

"If you can find it." My voice sounds as tired and defeated as I'm beginning to feel.

"Well, if it truly is enchanted, that shouldn't be too difficult. . . ."

She shuffles around in the dark. "I think I found it," she says, scooting so close she's practically sitting on top of me.

She thrusts the parchment first into my shoulder, then into my hand. "Sorry, can't see a thing." She laughs. "It's weird how it really doesn't feel like much. Just seems like an ordinary piece of paper to me."

"It is," I say. "Until you wish on it, and then it becomes what you need it to be."

"Oh, so it's wishing paper," Frankie says, as though that's an actual thing.

I press the paper between my palms. "It's more like manifesting paper," I tell her, remembering how it worked before. "You need to go through a series of steps, but yeah, wishing is part of that process."

"So, what should we wish for?" Frankie asks.

"I guess the first thing we should ask for is light."

The next thing I know, Frankie gasps as the page sparks to life and the whole room is illuminated.

TWENTY-EIGHT

3-D MOVIE

"Wow!" Frankie's gaze glints with awe as she glances between the paper and me. "So what happens next? You said it can become whatever you need it to be. Does that mean it can transform into something that will help us break free?"

"Not exactly," I say. "Or at least, it hasn't so far. I've only used it one other time, as a map to find my way here."

She leans back to better scrutinize me. "Why would anyone ask to come here?"

"I didn't ask to come here, but rather to the outside world, and this is where I ended up."

She regards me carefully. "So you all know about us, but we don't know about you?"

"Some people know about us," I say. "But most just think we're a legend. They don't believe such a place can really exist. But in our schools, we're taught a basic overview of your world. It leaves most people hoping they'll never have to come here. It would be impossible to fit in, and from what I've seen so far, fitting in is really important."

Frankie quietly thinks it over, then taps an index finger against the scroll. "So what should we wish for?"

I take a moment to consider. It seems like there's an unlimited number of things I could use. But the Seer warned that in the outside world, magic comes with a price. And since she never revealed what the price may be, I'm reluctant to rely on it too much.

"How about answers?" My gaze meets Frankie's. "What if we just ask it to show us whatever it thinks we need to know most at this exact moment?"

Frankie presses her lips into a thin, grim line. After mulling it over, she motions for me to proceed.

I go through the steps, and a moment later, Frankie exclaims, "Whoa, dude—this is legit!"

I open my eyes to find a three-dimensional holographic scene taking shape before me.

It's the image of a room—a nursery, to be exact. The walls are painted sky-blue, the ceiling is white, and the floor is dark hardwood with a cream-colored rug placed in the center. Against the far wall, there's an elaborate white crib with a baby inside. He gurgles contentedly as he makes his stuffed animals dance all around him using only his mind.

"He's so cute and lifelike!" Frankie says.

Tentatively, she moves toward him. But when she tries to touch the crib, her hand cuts right through the image and she squeals and backs away.

"I've never seen anything like this before," she whispers. "Not up close and in person, anyway. Have you?"

I shake my head and continue watching. I'm too awe-struck to speak.

A woman enters the room, takes the baby from the crib, and carries him into a brightly lit kitchen to feed him. But before she can even get the spoon to his mouth, the baby bends it with his mind and the food falls straight into his mother's lap.

"Hil-*arious*!" Frankie jostles her shoulder against mine and slaps her knee.

But all I can think is it's just like the stories I heard about Ollie. Only it's not Ollie. And the next scene confirms it when the baby stretches and grows. His arms and legs extend to the point where his joints repeatedly pop in and out of place, until the growing phase halts, and he's morphed into a full-sized man.

With his wavy blond hair, brown eyes, olive complexion,

and a tweed jacket I recognize from pictures, there's no doubt in my mind we're looking at a hologram of Yegor Quiver.

"I know him," I whisper. "That's the founder of Quiver Hollows."

Frankie glances between the hologram and me. "Don't you already know the history of your town? Why would the scroll show you what you already know?"

I shrug. "I get the feeling a few details might've been skipped."

We watch as the holographic depiction of Yegor sprints across the top of a rapidly spinning globe.

"Pretty sure that's symbolic," Frankie says. "Because no way is that possible."

"He was the most renowned spoon bender in the world," I tell her.

The globe-spinning scene switches to one with Yegor standing on a stage before a large crowd of people showering him with praise. Which leads me to wonder why he went looking for another life when the one we've seen so far looks pretty great.

"So, Yegor was like a celebrity?" Frankie turns to me for confirmation, but before I can answer, the scene disappears and the whole room goes black.

"What the—" Frankie grabs the scroll and gives it a couple of good shakes, to no avail. "It stopped working," she groans.

A second later, the room lights up again as a tall, lumbering man jumps from the shadows and Frankie and I both scream in terror.

We cower against the wall, watching as this larger-than-life fiend charges right toward us. His eyes blaze with fury as he hurls a stream of insults and throws a punch that narrowly misses Frankie's jaw.

"What the heck?" Frankie freezes, too afraid to move.

I grab hold of her arm and drag her to the other side of the room. But it's only a second later when the man has made it there too.

Trapped within the four metal walls, we zigzag back and forth across the space as the angry blue-eyed, black-haired hologram gives chase.

I remind myself he's not real. That he can't actually harm us. But he's so big and mean-looking that panic overrides common sense.

We're running in circles, practically screaming our heads off, when suddenly, Yegor reappears, and the strange, scary man goes after him instead.

"Faker!" he shouts. "Charlatan! Phony!" He jabs a finger right in Yegor's face, but Yegor ignores him.

Frankie and I huddle in a corner, struggling to catch our breath. "Do you know him?" Her voice quavers uncertainly.

I need a moment before I can speak. I'm still shaken by

the holographic attack. "I don't," I finally tell her. "Though he does look kind of familiar."

I rack my brain, trying to remember where I've seen him or someone like him, but I'm too agitated to think clearly.

We watch, frozen, as the big lumbering guy terrorizes Yegor all over the globe. For every article or book Yegor publishes, his nemesis quickly follows with a scathing review or a rebuttal piece of his own.

And so it goes, on and on through the years. Yegor and his nemesis age before our eyes, but nothing really changes until the day Yegor decides to pursue his longtime dream of discovering the legendary Land of Fog, Clouds, and Mist.

With his nemesis close on his trail, Yegor meets with shamans, tribal leaders, monks, and other explorers, but no one is able to help.

The scene fizzles out for a moment as the images begin to pixilate and diminish. Then, just when I'm sure the show is over, a new image of Yegor napping by a lake takes shape.

"Not sure how this is relevant, but okay . . ." Frankie smirks.

A gentle breeze stirs and the scent of flowers swirls all around us. A bright blue feather falls from the sky and tickles the tip of Yegor's nose as a disembodied voice whispers: *"All that is hidden hides in plain sight."*

The air crackles and sparks. An onslaught of blue feathers appears out of nowhere and rains down all around us, only to vanish a few moments later.

"I got chills!" Frankie hugs her waist. Before us, Yegor jumps up, smacks his forehead dramatically, and resumes his journey. A short time later, he's confronted by a glistening dome of fog, clouds, and mist.

"That's home." I lean closer, my heart racing at the sight. Like Frankie, I'm tempted to reach out and touch it. Maybe even try to immerse myself in it. But I know it's not real, so I stay put.

Yegor blinks at the shimmering, vaporous wall like he can hardly believe what he sees.

Beside me, Frankie sucks in a breath as I stare slack-jawed and mesmerized. This is the moment Yegor founded our town. This is the moment Quiver Hollows became the place I've always known it to be.

Yegor takes one step forward, then another. The third sees him entering a world where the air sparkles. Waterfalls zoom up and down, shooting from the bottom to the top, then back again like a zipper. It leaves us covered in a sheen of mist that instantly evaporates.

"Did you feel that?" Frankie runs a hand over her hair and studies her palm, looking for evidence that it really did happen.

I motion toward the ground, where a fluffle of blue bunnies hop toward us. Their pink noses twitch as they sniff the toes of our shoes. Frankie squeals with delight and kneels down to pet one, but a moment later, they're gone.

"Seriously? That's home?" Frankie hooks a thumb toward the hologram. "That's where you come from? Why would you ever leave a place like that?"

"Because it's not like that anymore," I say, hating the way the words feel on my tongue.

Our eyes meet for a moment; then I turn away and focus back on the show.

Yegor, eager to celebrate his discovery, steps back through the veil and shares the news with his nemesis. "I've discovered the Land of Fog, Clouds, and Mist!" he declares. "And it's even more beautiful than I imagined it would be!"

His nemesis, of course, merely smirks in reply.

So Yegor grabs him by the hand and yanks him inside.

"None of this is possible!" his nemesis shouts, refusing to even give it a chance. "You put something in my water! You tricked me!" His voice booms so loudly Frankie and I edge back toward the wall, fearing he'll become unhinged once again.

Yegor stands his ground. "How can you possibly deny all that's before you?" He stretches an arm wide, urging his nemesis to see the wonder that surrounds him.

With a show of reluctance, he takes a good look around, then turns to Yegor and exclaims, "We're going to be rich!" He punches the sky with his fist. If he sees Yegor's look of despair, he doesn't seem to care. "Do you have any idea how much money there is to be made? This could become the world's most famous amusement park!"

He rambles on about the proper placement of buildings, vendors, rides, and adjoining shops and hotels. Until they come upon a group of people quietly enjoying a late-afternoon picnic on a vast turquoise-tinged lawn.

Only these are no ordinary people. Some have tails, some have scales, and some have noses so long they look more like beaks.

Frankie nudges me, but I just lean forward. I've never heard this part of the story.

A beautiful girl covered in shimmering blue scales rises to introduce herself, and just like that, all talk of exploiting the land is replaced by nervous ramblings as Yegor's nemesis awkwardly introduces himself.

"I'm—I'm Vitaly," he stammers. "Vitaly Moonsliver."

Frankie gasps, her eyes bugging out as she slaps a hand over her mouth.

I sit frozen, too stunned to speak. My mind races as I try to piece it together, figure out what it all means and why the scroll wants me to know this.

"The Moonslivers name all their kids either Boris or Vitaly," Frankie whispers. "So it's impossible to know how far back this goes."

Before us, the beautiful woman smiles shyly, and says, "I'm Maris." A second later, the hologram grows blurry. The images speed past like someone pushed the fast-forward button. I catch a glimpse of Yegor teaching classes in spoon bending and other mystical arts as Vitaly and Maris marry and eagerly await the arrival of their firstborn child.

"Everyone seems so happy." Frankie gestures toward the scene of the townspeople celebrating Yegor by placing a statue of him in the middle of the town square. "What could have changed that?"

She's barely finished the question when the image warps and wavers, filling with static before it switches to one of Vitaly enraged.

Frankie turns to me. "Did I miss something?" she whispers.

I shrug. I'm as lost as she is. No one ever told me this part of Quiver Hollows's history.

There's a brief clip of a red-faced crying baby.

Followed by another clip of someone pulling a sheet over a body. Judging by the scales, I'm guessing it's Maris.

Then, from seemingly out of nowhere, a cry of heart-piercing grief explodes through the room, prompting the walls to shake and the floor to tremble as Frankie and I cup our hands over our ears and shudder in fear.

"What is that?" Frankie winces.

I nod toward the space just behind her, where Moonsliver looms, seething with rage.

We leap to our feet and rush to the far corner, putting as

much distance between us and him as possible. Still, there's no escaping his anger.

"What good is magic if it can't save the people you love?" he shouts from the depths of his belly. "How is this even possible when so many of you live well into your hundreds?"

He glares at an invisible crowd, making it seem as though he's glaring at us. As though he blames us for the death of his wife.

"You tricked me into believing in the very thing I've spent a lifetime debunking!"

Vitaly continues the rant, his words becoming increasingly caustic. A moment later the ground beneath him begins to quake as a wind kicks up that threatens to knock us right off our feet. Frankie grabs hold of my sleeve to keep from flying away.

"What's happening?" she cries, her fingers digging into my arm. "What's—"

Before she can finish, we watch as Vitaly is completely uprooted, his feet rising off the ground like I've seen Ming's do a thousand times before. Only, Moonsliver doesn't hover. He spins and whirls and soars ever higher, until, just like that, he's sucked right out of the world.

As quickly as it started, the wind halts and Frankie falls limp by my side.

"Where'd he go?" Breathlessly, she stares up at the roof, then back at me. "It's like, one second he was there"—she extends a skinny arm and points a shaky finger—"and the next— *Poof!* Gone! Have you ever seen anything like that?"

She stares at me, but I'm too busy watching the blank space where a moment ago, Vitaly Moonsliver stood. But just like Vitaly vanished from Quiver Hollows, the holographic movie we've been watching vanishes too.

I sink to the ground beside her. Try to make sense of everything I just saw. It's a lot to process, and in some ways, it leaves me with more questions than answers.

Why was this kept a secret for so long?

Am I the only one who didn't know?

My thoughts are interrupted when Frankie shakes my shoulder and says, "Grimsly—look!"

On the far wall a string of letters appear, one at a time, as though typed on an old-fashioned typewriter. We can even hear the punch of the keys being pressed, along with the ding of the bell on every return.

"'As people of magic know, words have power,'" Frankie reads. "'And the words Vitaly spoke the day he vanished created a curse so monstrous that every generation thereafter was doomed to suffer, no matter which side of the veil it was from.'"

Frankie's startled look matches my own.

"'While Vitaly resumed his life of cynicism and debunking, he was never able to locate Quiver Hollows again.'" I clear my throat, struggling to read every word before it's too late. The moment each sentence is completed, it vanishes, making room for the next. "'Though that didn't stop him from trying. While Vitaly never fell in love again (he no longer believed in such lies), he did go on to father more offspring—all of them boys, all of them losing their mother during childbirth. To every son born, Vitaly repeated the story of the wild trip he'd once made, and his sons did the same when they became fathers. Until generations of Moonslivers had all pledged a vow of revenge on Quiver Hollows in the name of their ancestor.'" I pause, allowing Frankie to take over.

"'Quiver Hollows had taken Vitaly's wife, his firstborn son, and, for a short time, his sanity by making him believe in the very thing he'd spent his life proving false. It was a terrible, terrible place, and one day, one of his descendants would find it, and make it pay for all the trouble it had caused.'" Frankie's voice quakes so badly, we tacitly agree to read the last words in silence.

While Vitaly's firstborn son went on to live a long and prosperous life in Quiver Hollows, he too was cursed.

Every woman he fell in love with eventually gave birth to a son, only to die in childbirth.

After a while, he too died a broken man.

And the same went for his sons.

Generations of Moonslivers, all of them falling victim to the same sad fate.

Until there were just three Moonslivers left on either side of the veil, destined to meet after all these years.

TWENTY-NINE

THE UGLY TRUTH

Frankie and I sit in silence, both of us too stunned to speak.

The holograph has disappeared.

The wall has gone blank.

But the story we witnessed is forever seared on my brain.

I'm a Moonsliver.

A direct descendant of Vitaly Moonsliver.

One of the last descendants of a long-cursed family.

My mother died in childbirth.

My father died shortly after.

The angry crowd claimed I came from a cursed family.

It's all the proof I need.

Which means that, for the last eleven years, Snelling has chosen to lie to me. Heck, the whole town has been in on the lie.

The question is why?

Was it to protect me from the truth?

Or was it something else entirely?

"Grimsly, you okay?" Frankie shoots me a concerned look, but I can barely bring myself to meet it.

I want to feel mad, but I'm not sure I should. Snelling has always done his best to protect me, even if it meant protecting me from the truth of my real family.

Is this the part of the conversation he chose to hold back the day he granted me Summerfield Lawn?

And if so, is it somehow connected to my being the Keeper?

Funny how I always wanted to feel like I belonged, only to discover that I actually *do* belong—to the worst sort of family I could ever imagine.

But at least now I know why I'm so glaringly normal.

My head is spinning. My body feels hollow, untethered, disjointed, and loose. It's like everything I thought I once knew about my world—about myself—has been flipped upside down.

"I'm a Moonsliver," I say, as though testing the words on my tongue. "I'm not a Summerfield at all."

"Maybe," Frankie whispers.

"Not maybe," I say. "For sure. I'm a Moonsliver. There's no getting around it."

"Still, it doesn't mean—" she starts.

"Doesn't mean what?"

"It doesn't mean that you're cursed."

I close my eyes. Yes, of course, the curse. It doesn't feel like much of a threat from where I sit now, since it's still a long ways away from playing out. But one day, when I do fall in love and start a family, it's pretty much guaranteed that my wife will die in childbirth and our son will thrive, only to relive the curse when it's his time.

"Curses can be broken," Frankie says.

"Can they?" I stare at her blindly. I feel so out of my league.

"Sure," she says, as though it's really that easy. "You just have to find the right reversal spell, that's all."

"If it was that simple, then why has it dragged on for so long?"

"I don't know," she admits, the air of confidence she wore just a moment ago swiftly diminishing. "But there's a way, Grimsly. There always is."

I nod. Maybe she's right. Then again, maybe she's not. Either way, it's hardly the biggest problem I face at the moment.

"I have my own confession to make." Frankie's words

take me by surprise. Though it's the shy look on her face that startles me most. "I knew about Quiver Hollows way before any of this."

I sit in stunned silence.

"The first time I was thrown into the hole, it was because I got caught sneaking into Moonsliver's office late one night. I was looking for some matches to light a candle for a spell I was working on, when I found a stack of old journals piled high on his desk. The things they revealed remind me a lot of the story we just saw. I was kind of in a hurry, since I didn't want to risk getting caught, though I did skim enough to see the name *Quiver Hollows* written multiple times, and I'm pretty sure the journals were written by Vitaly Moonsliver. Probably the same Vitaly Moonsliver we just saw. Anyway, I was just about to leave with the matches shoved in my pocket and one of the journals tucked in my waistband when Headmaster Moonsliver caught me and tossed me in here."

"How long were you in for?"

"Almost two weeks. I thought I would die. I'm pretty sure he wanted me to die, which is why I fought so hard to live."

"Who let you out?"

"One of the cleaning crew." She frowns. "Only it was by accident. They thought they'd be retrieving my body, when, *surprise!*" She shakes her head as a sour expression washes over her face. "But, Grimsly—" Her eyes find mine. "There's something you need to know. The boy who was bullying you?"

"The one with the metal teeth?" I ask.

"No," she says. "And by the way, those are called braces, and his name is Fogbottom. Henry Fogbottom."

"The one with the red spots?"

"That's called acne, and no, not him either. That's Wolfhart. Samuel Wolfhart. I'm talking about the other one—the one who kind of looks like you. His name is Boris—"

Before she can finish, I whisper the truth. "Boris Moonsliver. My cousin." It takes a moment for the gravity of the truth to sink in. Once it does, I'm not sure why it took me so long to see it. It all makes perfect sense. "He's the boy with the fake lobster-claw hands," I tell her. "He's the bone thief. He stole the bones right out of the graves and brought them all here. And he didn't just happen to find me when I crawled out from the tunnel. He was waiting for me. He *baited* me like a fish and lured me right into his world."

Finally, all the pieces of the puzzle have fallen into place. There's just one remaining question in need of an answer.

"But why did they steal the bones?" I search Frankie's face. "What are they doing with them? What's the purpose of bringing them here?"

Frankie's gaze holds mine. "You're not going to like this," she says.

THIRTY

REVENGE AGENDA

"So far, I don't like any of it, but I still need to know." I watch as Frankie paces the room, lit only by the dull glow provided by the enchanted scroll.

"They're grinding the bones and using the resulting dust as a *supplement*." She wiggles her fingers, adding air quotes around the last word.

I stare at her, not quite following.

"They're eating it."

I gape. There's no way I heard right. "Who's eating it? And how could you possibly know?"

"The Moonslivers are eating it. I didn't really put it together until now. Or at least, I didn't know what it was. But yeah, after seeing them grinding the bones into powder, I'm pretty positive that's what they're doing with it."

I scramble to my feet. "But *why?*" I ask. "Why would anyone do that? What would be the point?" I start to pace in the opposite direction, the two of us meeting in the middle, then heading to the far sides of the room before spinning around and meeting again. All the while my mind races, searching for plausible explanations for what this might mean if it turns out to be true.

"I know it sounds crazy," Frankie says. "But hear me out. Ever since Moonsliver discovered I survived the hole, he's made me work in the family's private chambers a few days a week."

I stop in my tracks. "Why would Moonsliver trust you in his own home?"

"Oh, I never claimed he trusts me," Frankie says. "I think it's more like that old saying: *Keep your friends close and your enemies closer.* Anyway, one of my duties is to work in their kitchen, doing their dishes and stuff, like a maid. Well, I noticed that on the table where they eat, they have this shaker. Not like a shaker for salt or pepper—it's a little bigger than that. More like the kind of shaker you use for grated parmesan cheese at an Italian restaurant."

My face remains blank.

"Okay, so you've never been to an Italian restaurant," she says. "Neither have I, but I've seen movies." She rolls her eyes. "Anyway, all you need to know is that they have a shaker, and inside that shaker is a fine ivory-colored powder that the family adds to all their meals. I even heard Moonsliver joke once and say something like *'Don't forget your pixie dust!'* And I peered around the corner and watched as Boris shook some of it onto his potatoes."

I rub my lips together. I can see where this is headed.

"Moonsliver acts like it's a protein supplement, meant to help keep them all strong, healthy, and alert."

"But it's really the ground-up bones they stole from Quiver Hollows!" I finish the statement for her. "But again, why? What would be the point?"

"Well," Frankie says, "let's walk through the facts as we know them. You got here from the drainpipe, right? I don't think that's how Boris got to Quiver Hollows. I think Vitaly's been feeding Boris a steady diet of bone dust since he was a kid. It's possible this goes back even further than you think."

I consider what she told me. It would certainly explain the placement of Yegor Quiver's statue and the tricky way we had to move it so I could find my way here. I remember at the time thinking how odd it seemed, and wondering if it had ever been breached in the past. Apparently, it had. Somehow, the Moonslivers had found their way back, and once it was discovered and the tunnel was sealed, they had to find a new way to enter.

"The bone dust is giving the Moonslivers magical powers?" I admit it's not really a question I'm expecting Frankie to answer. It's more like I'm thinking out loud and trying the words to see if they fit. Turns out they fit perfectly. Suddenly, it all falls into place. "The bones are magic!" My voice trills with excitement.

Frankie stares at me blankly.

"As you saw in the hologram, there's nothing ordinary about the animals in Quiver Hollows. So the day Snelling let me turn Summerfield Lawn into a pet cemetery, it was under the condition that I protect the bones at all costs. And though he never got around to explaining why, I know without a doubt it was about keeping the bones where they belong."

Frankie cocks her head in question. "Can you catch me up? I'm a little lost here."

"I'm the Keeper—the Keeper of the bones. The bones contain the magic that binds the town. I think the job fell to me the day Snelling found me in Summerfield Lawn surrounded by bunnies. I was two years old at the time, and to this day, no one knows how I got there."

Frankie's eyebrows rise halfway up her forehead, but she gestures for me to continue.

"When Boris started to steal the bones, the magic began

to disappear, causing the town to become normal, like everywhere else. It's the animal bones that make Quiver Hollows mystical, quirky, and weird. Now that all the bones are gone, the town is in complete normal chaos. It was my job to ensure they remained undisturbed so that the town would stay abnormal."

I think about it for a moment, and then I look at her and say, "But what I don't understand is why Vitaly would choose to give Boris magical powers when he's a self-proclaimed debunker of magic."

"Because," Frankie responds, "he's read the journals, and he knows that magic is real. Heck, if nothing else, there's no denying the curse that's haunted his family for all these years. The thing is, magic is empowering. It allows people greater control over their lives and their destinies. Magic allows for endless choice and variety. And for someone as controlling and power-hungry as Vitaly, who wants everyone to be the same, think the same, look the same, and do exactly as he says, magic is one of the world's greatest threats. So what better way to make sure the rest of us never even get a chance to get near it than by brainwashing us into thinking magic only exists in the minds of the pathetic and weak?"

I sit with her words. They all ring true.

"Also, I'm pretty sure he's preparing to go after you. He's been watching you ever since you arrived. He knows you're not from New York."

"But still, why me? I don't have any magic."

"You sure about that?" Frankie cocks her head.

"Trust me, I'm the most boring, normal person in all of Quiver Hollows, which was part of the problem. I didn't leave voluntarily. I was practically run out of town."

"Well, then it's working, isn't it?" she says.

I stop pacing long enough to study her.

"Because here's how I see it: They gave Boris the power to enter Quiver Hollows by feeding him the bone dust starting when he was a kid. He slipped back in to steal more bones. And this time he took so many it started siphoning the magic from the town. Once everyone noticed the changes, they blamed you—the one person who's not like them. The plan worked perfectly, if you ask me."

"You sound like you admire him."

"Not at all." Frankie shakes her head. "But if you want to beat the villain at his own game, then you need to outsmart him, and that begins by learning how to think like he does."

"I'm not sure I could."

"Why? Because you're too pure of heart?" Frankie laughs. "C'mon, Grimsly, you said so yourself—you're not magical. And, well, neither is Boris or Vitaly. But what's the one thing Moonsliver wants the most? What is he after?"

"Revenge," I say, without even thinking it through. "He wants to avenge his loss, his reputation, himself, the fates of his ancestors. So he's infected every generation with his hatred for Quiver Hollows, not realizing that they alone are responsible—that it was the Moonslivers, not Quiver Hollows, who brought the curse on themselves."

I realize I keep using the word *them*, like I'm not one of them.

As though I'm somehow distanced from it all.

As though I'm not a Moonsliver too.

But if Frankie notices, she doesn't let on. "Sounds about right to me." She grins. "Now the question remains: What are we going to do about it?"

"We?"

"Well, sure," she says. "You don't think I plan to stick around here, do you? Quiver Hollows looks amazing, and as soon as this is handled, you're taking me with you."

THIRTY-ONE

LIGHT AS A FEATHER

While Snelling may have never succeeded in teaching me the art of spoon bending, he did instill in me, from a very young age, the idea that everything is useful in more than one way. And I mean *everything*. Even the worst, most embarrassing, most humiliating moment of your life can be turned into a learning experience if you're willing to look at it from a fresh new angle.

The same goes for objects.

With this in mind, I reconsider the things I brought with me, this time viewing them with a more open mind.

Suddenly the bent spoon Ollie gave me at the start of my journey isn't just a bent spoon anymore—it might also prove to be a way out of this place. Unfortunately, it's on the wrong side of the wall.

"What're you doing?" Frankie asks as I head for the door and try to pry it open with my bare hands, which of course doesn't work.

"Hold that paper up just a little higher," I say. Luckily the scroll continues to radiate just enough light for me to navigate.

Frankie hovers close by, keeping the paper in my line of sight as I walk the small space, searching for a way to escape. But the metal is smooth and thick, and the only way out is the same way we entered.

Frustrated, I step toward the center and roll my neck until I'm staring up at the roof, remembering how I watched the hologram of Moonsliver swirl out of here.

"Frankie," I say. "What's up there?"

She turns the paper until it reveals what looks to be a small skylight built high into the ceiling.

"It's a hole at the top of the hole," she says. "Just another torture device. During the day, the sun shines down relentlessly and there's no escape. When it's raining, it floods. When it snows, don't get me started. A person could freeze to death, and it's rumored to have happened before."

I turn to look at her, an idea forming.

"Did you eat the bone dust?"

She rubs her lips together, as though weighing whether she should answer.

"When you work in the Moonslivers' kitchen, do you ever steal a few extra pinches here and there? And if so, how much?"

I study her closely. Frankie is skinny—some might even say underweight. And from yesterday, she barely ate anything off her tray. Yet she must be eating something, somewhere, or else she wouldn't be standing here now.

"I eat a lot of it," she confesses. "I mean, I didn't know where it came from until now, which makes me feel bad. But I thought, why should the Moonslivers get all the good stuff and force us to eat gross, lumpy gruel—it's not fair! So yeah, I steal that, and a lot of their normal food too. Why do you ask? What are you getting at?" Her tone edges toward defensive.

"I'm just thinking—and I know it'll probably sound crazy—but I have this feather that Ming gave me." I retrieve the pink feather from the place where Moonsliver dropped it.

"And?" Frankie shoots a skeptical look between the feather and me. "Can this Ming person fly or something? Because if you're thinking what I think you're thinking—"

"Not exactly." I cut her off. "But Ming can levitate really, really high. . . ."

"And you're hoping that the feather—that tiny pink girly

feather—will help me levitate all the way to the top of the building so I can soar through the skylight?"

"I know it sounds dumb." I start doubting the feather enough to dunk it back into my bag, when Frankie grins and snatches it right out of my hand.

"Not dumb at all!" She waves it between us. "But once I'm outside, how will I get you out too?"

"Oh, no," I say. "Make no mistake, I'm coming with you."

"Uh, that's unlikely." Frankie frowns.

"What's that supposed to mean?"

She wiggles the feather just under my nose. "It's a feather, Grimsly, not a helicopter. Heck, it's not even a full set of wings. It's one single feather. I mean, seriously, how much faith are you putting in this thing? Not to mention you're twice my size."

"I refuse to give up without at least trying."

"Fine," she agrees. "We'll give it a shot, but if it doesn't work, then what? You'll still be stuck inside."

I get to pacing again when I remember the spoon Moon-sliver tossed onto the lawn. It was one of the many baby spoons Ollie bent as a kid, and since everyone knows that young magic is the most potent magic . . .

"The spoon!" I say. "You use it to pick the lock."

Frankie shoots me a doubtful look. "If it's still out there, that is."

"It will be," I assure her, but mostly because I need to believe it. I have no way of knowing for sure.

Without another word she holds the feather high, crouches low, and leaps into the air. And wouldn't you know it, the feather lifts her halfway to the ceiling, where she hovers for a moment. When I try to grab ahold of her foot and go with her, we both come crashing right down.

"So . . ." She scrambles to her feet and kicks off her shoes. "Now that I've proven my point, how about a leg up so I can get a better liftoff?"

I kneel down far enough so that she can climb onto my back; then I rise on shaky knees as her toes grip my shoulders hard.

"Find your center," I whisper when Frankie wobbles precariously for a few nerve-racking moments.

Once she's righted herself, she says, "On the count of three. One . . . two . . ."

On three, she springs toward the sky, and I watch for one dazzling moment as the feather carries her all the way through the skylight and into the night.

THIRTY-TWO

SKELETON KEY

Waiting is the hardest.

It feels like each passing second swells into an hour.

Since the moment Frankie disappeared through the roof, I've stood with my ear pressed hard against the door, alert to any sign or sound of her picking the lock, only to feel my heart crash in despair when all remains quiet on the other side of the shed.

Have I misjudged her?

Is she now, powered on bone dust and the knowledge of

everything that's been revealed, on her way to Quiver Hollows, leaving me behind to wither and die without a second thought?

I push hard against the door, bang on it with both fists, and give it a good solid kick, mostly out of frustration. I already know from the prior kicks that no good will come of it.

"Frankie!" I whisper. That whisper soon rises to a scream when I repeat: "Frankie!"

I sink to the ground in a fury of rage and betrayal, when I hear the deadbolt turn in the lock and the door shoves open, butting hard against my back.

"Did you seriously doubt me?" Frankie stands in the doorway and scowls.

"Yes," I say, seeing no use denying the truth.

"Well, lesson learned." She grins. "I'm loyal and trustworthy. Now let's get out of here. And move quietly. The last thing we want is for Moonsliver to know we're on the run."

"But where exactly are we running?" I ask. "I can't go back to Quiver Hollows—not without the bones."

"There are no bones," she reminds me. "It's all bone dust now."

"Then fine, not without the bone dust. It's imperative that I return with it. Otherwise, there's no point to any of this."

"I'm not sure that's possible," she says. "There are too

many barrels of the stuff, far too many for us to handle alone. And besides, how are you going to drag it through the tunnel? Seriously, it would take a whole army of people to help us, and believe me, you're my only friend here. There's no one I can recruit. No one I can trust. They're all too afraid of Moonsliver to risk turning on him."

"Fine," I say, though the truth is, it's anything but. I recognize a temporary defeat when I see one. "Then for now, we'll need a place to hide until we can figure something out."

I start to head for the tunnel, trying not to think about all the spiders and bats and other night crawlers that inhabit that place, when Frankie says, "Don't you think the tunnel is the first place they'll check once they discover us missing?"

I stop in my tracks. She makes a good point. Still, it's the only logical place I can think of.

"I know another, much better place," she says.

"I thought you said there are no hiding places here."

"I did." She shrugs, leading the way as we race through the dark, our feet sliding across the dew-covered lawn. "But the best place to hide is in plain sight." She slows when she reaches our building, then pulls me around the back toward the trellis that leads to her second-floor room. "I sneak out a lot," she explains.

"What about your roommate?"

"Don't have one. She was sent to the hole and was never seen again."

With Frankie close on my heels, I climb the trellis, then duck through her window. As I stand in the center of her darkened room, I instantly regret my decision to go along with this plan.

"As long as Moonsliver thinks we're in the hole, he won't think to look here." She does her best to reassure me, but I'm not sure I agree.

I feel so visible, so exposed. With only the flimsiest wooden door and no lock to protect us, the odds of being discovered veer dangerously high.

"Go on, have a seat." Frankie gestures to the bed opposite hers. I'm just lowering myself onto the mattress when I notice a fake lobster-claw hand placed on the pillow.

Only this time, I don't scream. By now I can recognize a fake severed hand when I see one.

I pinch it between my fingers, hold it before me, and say, "Care to explain?"

Frankie stares impassively. Doesn't so much as flinch. Which seems like a pretty abnormal reaction when first confronted with such a thing.

"That's not mine." The words come quickly. A little too quickly.

I want to believe her, really I do, but I'm not sure I should.

"What's it doing here—in your room—if it's not yours?" I continue to wave the hand at her.

She shrugs but keeps silent.

"Have you seen it before?"

"Have you?" She glares.

"You know I have," I say. "Question is, what is it doing here?"

She works her jaw, probably dreaming up a reply, a way out of this mess. Suddenly, the door springs open, and my roommate and tormentor, Henry Fogbottom, walks in.

He takes one look at us and freezes, his gaze darting between Frankie and me and the fake lobster-claw hand. "Sewer Swine? Spell Spinner?" he says. "You're not supposed to be here."

"And you are?" Frankie's tone is tough, and to my amazement, he really does seem afraid of her.

He shoots a nervous look down the hall, then quietly closes the door and presses his back flush against it. "Listen," he whispers. "You've got to help me find a way out of here."

Frankie shakes her head, rolls her eyes, and pretends to ignore him.

"I'm serious, I don't want any part of this. Never did."

"Is this yours?" I wave the hand before him.

He shakes his head but holds my gaze. "It belongs to Boris. He has a bunch of them. He told me to put it in your bed, I guess to scare you or something."

"So you put it in my room instead?" Frankie frowns.

"I heard you both got sent to the hole, so I've been hiding in here ever since. I figured they wouldn't look for me here."

"Why would they be looking for you?"

"Because I'm not a bunny killer, man. I just—I won't do it. There's no way they can make me."

"What?" Frankie and I blurt out, our voices overlapping.

He looks distraught, his gaze dark and feverish. "They've got these—these crazy bunnies that they keep in cages down in the lab. They're all colorful too, you know. Like crazy colors. The kind not normally found in nature."

"Like blue, pink, orange, and green?" I say.

"Yellow too!" He rakes a hand through his hair. "They ran a bunch of experiments on them—stuff that's too sick to mention. And then they made them multiply, and when the old ones died, they ground up their bones."

Frankie and I trade a meaningful look.

"So you know?" He glances between us and rubs a hand over his face. "Anyway," he continues, "it wasn't long before the rabbits stopped multiplying and they all started dying. No matter what Moonsliver did, he couldn't keep them alive. Then, before too long, there's a whole new batch of bunnies, and all you have to do is look in their eyes to see how frightened they are. I seriously think some of them are dying from shock or fear or whatever. All I know for sure is it's not good, not good at all. And the ones that don't die quickly enough for Moonsliver, he's ordering us to kill them so he can grind up their bones while they're still fresh. It's like—he's gone nuts with the bone dust, and I don't want any part of it. He's ordering us to kill them all, even the babies. Especially the babies."

"Because young magic is the most potent magic," I say, not realizing at first that I've spoken out loud until I see the way they react to my words. "The bones are magic," I tell him.

"Whatever, bro. Look, all I know is that I am not at all down with this. I don't want any part of the Skeleton Crew."

"You didn't seem to have any problem when it came to tormenting me." I fix my gaze on his, practically daring him to look away.

He runs his tongue across the front of his teeth and fidgets uncomfortably. "Listen . . ." He squints at my hair, then drops his gaze to stare at his shoes. "I'm sorry about that. Truly. But you don't understand how it is here. You're either a victim or—"

"Or a bully," Frankie finishes for him. "Is that what you were going to say?"

He shrugs, but I notice he can't bring himself to meet her gaze.

"You know that's a load of nonsense, right?" Frankie will not back down. "I've been here almost as long as you and I didn't choose sides. Most people don't. We're all just trying to survive. It's people like you who make this place even more miserable than it already is. It's the mindless minions who give bullies their power. Think about that next time you decide to join forces with a tyrant."

He shifts his weight from foot to foot and says, "You're right. I know."

"Where's Moonsliver now?" I ask, eager to move on to a topic that's a little more urgent.

He looks at me. "Gone. He and Boris went to get more bunnies."

I look at Frankie and Frankie looks at me.

"We need to leave," I say. "Now! Before it's too late!"

"But not without me—right? You're taking me with you!" He clings to the door, refusing to let us exit without him.

"Fine, Fogbottom," Frankie agrees. "But only if you promise to not get in the way, to make yourself useful, and to start calling people by their real names."

THIRTY-THREE

MEMENTO MORI

We walk boldly through the halls. With both Moonslivers gone, there's no longer any need to worry about getting caught.

Or at least, that's what we think until we turn a corner and Samuel Wolfhart bolts out of the darkness and steps into our path.

"Where the heck do you think you're going?" he asks.

I'm about to reply, when Fogbottom grabs Frankie by the elbow and punches me hard in the arm. "Keeping these two out of trouble," he says.

215

Wolfhart stays rooted in place and studies our group with a distrustful gaze. "Thought they were sent to the hole?"

"They were," Fogbottom insists, his tone edged with the kind of authority that takes me aback. When I first came across him, he seemed like the weakest link in the group. And in a sense, maybe the fact that he's helping us now only proves that he is. If he's actually helping us, that is. Nothing here is ever what it seems, and I can't shake the feeling that every move I make could lead to a trap.

"You let 'em out?" Wolfhart steps closer, his face pinched in a way that's meant to be menacing. And even though he's outnumbered, strangely, it works.

"Course not," Fogbottom scoffs, but the way his voice catches betrays just how nervous he is.

"Then how'd they get out?" Wolfhart glances between us.

"Who the heck knows?" Fogbottom adopts an annoyed tone. "You'll have to ask them. But later, not now. I'm kind of in a hurry, bro."

"And exactly where are you in a hurry to?" Wolfhart refuses to budge. "You working with them?"

He's on to us. Really, truly on to us.

"Don't be an idiot," Fogbottom says.

"He can't help it," Frankie cuts in. "He was born that way."

She jerks free of Fogbottom's grip as Wolfhart rushes

her, his outraged face glowing orange under the dim golden glow of the security lights.

Instinctively, I wedge myself between them. Me, of all people. I've never been in a fight in my life. "Back off, Wolfhart." I stare him straight in the eye, refusing to yield until he looks away.

Inside, I admit, I'm not feeling nearly as confident as I may come across. Still, I hang in there. After all, I'm the Keeper. I have a mission to fulfill. And there's no way this misguided bully will stand in my way.

I guess it works, because soon after, Wolfhart says, "What're you doing?" He looks imploringly at Fogbottom. "Why are you working with them?"

"Because I'm tired of working for Moonsliver," he says. "I quit. I'm done. And if you're smart, you'll join us."

"You'll never get away with it." Wolfhart glares. "It's just a matter of time before the Moonslivers return and—"

"*If* they return."

All eyes turn to Fogbottom.

"I'm not so sure they're coming back."

"What makes you say that?" I ask. It's bad enough to imagine them visiting Quiver Hollows. Their planning to stay is unthinkable.

"Listen, I don't know for sure. But—" His eyes dart up and down the length of the hallway. "Aw, whatever. I don't know why I'm still protecting them. I guess it's just the lingering effects of Moonsliver brainwashing. . . ."

"Get to the point!" Frankie cries, which is pretty much the same thing I'm thinking.

Fogbottom squares his gaze on hers. "Pretty sure they laid off the staff. When I was on my way to hide out in your room, I saw a bunch of faculty leaving. They were hauling their belongings like they were going for good."

"So they're just going to abandon us here?" Frankie is outraged. "They're just going to leave us locked in this place so we can starve to death?"

"That's the gist." Fogbottom shrugs.

"And you're still siding with them?" Frankie whirls on Wolfhart and gives him a scathing look. "How gullible are you?"

"How gullible are *you*?" he shoots back. "You don't even know if any of that's true." Wolfhart does his best to defend himself, but Frankie rolls her eyes and scowls in return. "He could be making it up!" He jabs a thumb in Fogbottom's direction.

"You're right," Frankie says. With her arms folded across her chest, her gaze pierces his. "Maybe he is lying. Either way, I'm not going to stick around to find out, are you?"

Wolfhart stands defiantly before us. And yet, you can practically hear the wheels grinding in his head as he weighs the long list of possible consequences.

After a few prolonged moments of silence, Frankie shoves him hard in the side. "If you won't do the right thing and join us, then at least don't slow us down." She leaves Wolfhart staring after us while she zooms down a maze of short and long hallways and Fogbottom and I race to catch up.

She pushes through a set of double doors and flies down two flights of stairs, where she pushes through another set of swinging double doors and leads us to a long, gloomy hallway with solid steel doors lining both sides.

"This reminds me of the cell." I stop in my tracks.

"I promise you, it's not the cell." When I don't move, Frankie says, "Trust me."

I glance at Fogbottom, figuring he should be able to confirm, seeing as how he's responsible for locking me in there.

"We're good," he assures me.

"Where are we going?" I ask, back to following Frankie. "And how do you know which one to open when they all look the same?"

"Not to mention that we don't have a key," echoes Fogbottom.

But Frankie remains undeterred. "Trust me," she repeats, stopping before a door bearing a brass plaque engraved with the words MEMENTO MORI.

She traces a finger over the letters as Fogbottom says, "What does it mean?"

"It's Latin," she whispers. "It translates to 'Remember you must die.'"

"As though someone could possibly forget?" Fogbottom makes a face.

"It's supposed to help people to remember to live fully in the life they've been given, or to stay on purpose, or to keep your ego in check and not get so full of yourself that you think you're invincible. Death is the greatest equalizer. Rich or poor, powerful or weak, genius or idiot—death comes for all of us eventually. Anyway, I'm pretty sure this is it," she says.

"What is it?" I ask. "What are you looking for?"

"You'll see." But when she tries the handle, the door is locked tight.

"Now what?" Fogbottom whines, glancing nervously down the hall, then back at Frankie.

Frankie thrusts an open hand toward me and barks, "Spoon, please!" like a surgeon at the start of an operation, asking the nurse for the scalpel in order to make the first cut.

I reach into my bag and dig out the spoon, having no good way of knowing whether it will work on this door like it did on the last.

Frankie gets to work, tries shoving it into the lock. But after a few frustrated attempts, she gives up.

In the not-so-far distance, we can hear a set of footsteps drawing near.

"I don't know what to do," Frankie says. "The spoon's not working, and honestly, I'm not even sure this is the right room!"

"Great!" Fogbottom frets. "Just great! I risked everything for you guys—and now, if I get caught because of you, I swear I'll—"

I grab the spoon from Frankie, pinch it by the bowl, and run the stem carefully between the door and the jamb. Working my way toward the bolt, I hold my breath and hope for a miracle as the footsteps continue to pound, growing closer and closer.

Frankie sucks in a breath.

Fogbottom continues his whispered litany of empty threats.

The two of them push and crowd to the point where I can barely see what I'm doing. Then the deadbolt retreats, the spoon slides clean, and I throw the door open and whisper, "Hurry!" ushering them inside before locking the door securely behind me.

THIRTY-FOUR

THE BONE PALACE

The first thing I notice when I enter the room are bones.

Lots and lots and lots of bones.

So many bones they seem to gather and swirl before my eyes—entire constellations consisting of skulls, femurs, tibias, fibulas, sacra, and mandibles. And with the walls painted the color of midnight, the bones stand out even more than they normally would.

There's a massive chandelier that hangs overhead and it's made entirely of phalanges, skulls, and individual vertebrae. The guttered candles embedded in them drip fat frozen tears of deep scarlet wax, lending a bloodied, beaten appearance, like the leftover evidence of some gruesome act.

Inside my head, my teeth rattle, and my heart thumps hard in my chest. *It's just wax, just bones,* I tell myself as my gaze travels across the room to a framed piece of bone art, made from broken bits of skeleton. My guess is it was purposely arranged to resemble the Moonsliver family crest.

I wander to the opposite end of the room, where, right in the center, sits a giant throne. With a deep red velvet cushion propped on its seat, its back is crafted entirely of ribs, while each armrest is crowned at the end with a skull.

"So creepy," Frankie whispers as Fogbottom stands just beside her, whistling quietly under his breath. The two of them are enthralled by the startlingly ghoulish sight, but my own reaction doesn't quite match.

It's not that the sight of so many bones leaves me frightened. If anything, I've learned that the living are far more harmful than the dead could ever be.

It's more that the sight leaves me feeling despondent in a way that not even failing the spoon-bending exam did.

As the Keeper, I never should've allowed this to happen.

This room is additional proof of my failure.

I climb the steps that lead to the throne and run my hand over the soft curve of the skulls, when suddenly it occurs to me that these aren't rabbit skulls.

They're not even animal skulls.

They're too big . . .

Too . . . humanlike . . .

With their human-shaped teeth . . .

"Um, guys." I quickly pull my hand away and frantically wipe it down the side of my pants as though it will erase the regret of having just touched that. "I think it's even worse than I thought," I tell them. "I think these are—"

From somewhere behind me, Frankie gasps, and I turn to find the door banging wide open as Wolfhart appears in the entry.

THIRTY-FIVE

PARTING GIFT

"You shouldn't be in here." Wolfhart stands in the doorway.

"Yeah, and what are you going to do about it?" Frankie places a hand on each bony hip and stares Wolfhart down. It's like watching a Chihuahua go after a bear; she has no concept of the staggering difference in size.

Wolfhart frowns and looks around uncertainly. "Let's just go, okay?" he finally says, jangling a set of keys in his hand. "This room gives me the creeps."

"You've been here before?" Fogbottom speaks in a way that sounds almost jealous.

He nods distractedly. "Once or twice, and I don't like it any better now."

"What's this about?" Frankie asks. "What's the point of this room?"

Wolfhart looks directly at me, and says, "Heck if I know." But it's clear that he's lying. "I thought you guys wanted to leave." He jangles the keys enticingly.

"We do," I say.

At the same time, Frankie says, "You don't even know how to drive."

Wolfhart shrugs. "How hard can it be? You turn the key, press your foot to the gas pedal, and steer."

"Pretty sure there's more to it than that." Frankie rolls her eyes.

Wolfhart is just about to protest when I say, "Tell me what you know about this room."

He shuffles uncertainly from foot to foot and scratches at a spot of acne on his cheek. "I told you I don't—"

"Stop lying," I say, "and prove we can trust you. Otherwise, you're on your own."

He remains by the door, weighing the odds. After a moment, he tucks the keys in his fist, steps forward, and says, "Everything here is made from bones."

"Obviously," Frankie groans.

"Only they're not animal bones."

I nod. Just as I thought.

"They're human bones."

"You mean like—from dead students? The ones who were sent to the hole and never returned?" Frankie's voice trills with panic.

"No. Those bodies get dumped in unmarked graves," Wolfhart says a little too easily for such an abhorrent statement. But I guess living in this place can desensitize a person.

"They're the bones of all the dead Moonsliver wives who died during childbirth!" I cry, having no real proof to back it up, yet somehow knowing it's true. "Because of the curse," I breathe the last part the same time as Frankie.

"So you know." Wolfhart's gaze darts between us.

"Know what?" Fogbottom frowns. "How come everyone here knows stuff but me? Why am I the only one left in the dark?"

"Later," I tell him, though it doesn't do much to placate him in the present. Then, returning to Wolfhart, I say, "So why did they keep the bones? Why did they memorialize them in this way? Why not just bury them like normal people do?"

"Because they're committed to never forgetting the price that they've paid. They're committed to seeking and getting revenge against the ones who did this to them."

"*Memento mori,*" Frankie whispers to no one in particular.

"They did it to themselves," I say. "The curse is on them."

"Try telling them that." Wolfhart works his jaw and runs

his tongue along the inside of his cheek, making an annoying clucking sound I wish he would stop.

While it's easy to get sidetracked by all the weirdness surrounding me, the fact is, Quiver Hollows is in trouble. Like, really deep trouble. Which means everyone I care about is in danger. And while I know I need to get there as soon as possible, and bring the bone dust along with me, I'm not sure how I'm supposed to go about accomplishing that. Frankie was right—there's no way I can haul it all through the drainpipe.

"Do you know where they are now?" I ask Wolfhart.

"Not exactly," he says, uttering the two last words I wanted to hear. "Though, see that over there?" He points toward the other side of the room.

"The family crest?" I say.

He shakes his head. "Not a family crest. They use it like a crystal ball. They have a way of reading the bones."

"How do you know all this?" Frankie asks as I race in that direction.

"You're not the only one who sneaks around and eavesdrops," he says.

"I thought they didn't believe in magic," Fogbottom says. "They've drilled that into our heads since day one!"

"They're liars. They do believe, they just don't want us to believe. And they've spent the last several generations searching for a way to break the curse. They're convinced their dead wives speak to them through the bones. They've developed a whole ritual around it."

"What's the ritual?" I ask. "And what exactly are they looking for when they read the bones?"

"I don't know the ritual," Wolfhart says. "I was never allowed in on that. But as far as what they're looking for— well, it would be a way to reverse the curse. It's all they really think about. Or, correction—there was a time when they were obsessed with finding a way back to the place where the curse started, but once they got that figured out, then it was all about the curse." He looks right at me. "Don't get me wrong, though; this isn't just about reversing the curse, it's also about destroying the place that's responsible for the curse."

And just like that, the rest of the pieces fall into place.

"By stealing the bones, they rid the town of magic," I say. "And they think that by killing the magic, the curse will be reversed."

Wolfhart nods. "That, and the town will be left exposed and destroyed and at the mercy of the Moonslivers."

I turn toward the piece I mistook for a family crest. Up close it looks like a mess of bones. When I move farther back, it looks pretty much the same.

"How do you read this thing?" I ask.

Wolfhart shrugs. "Afraid I can't help you with that."

I look at Frankie and Fogbottom, but they just shake their heads.

So I pull the enchanted scroll from my bag, press my palm to it, and go through the motions.

I'm several minutes in when Frankie says, "Uh, Grimsly, it's not working."

She's right. The paper is blank.

Is this what the Seer meant when she warned that magic comes at a price?

That it can only be used a few times before it quits?

I reach for the feather, wave it around, but again, nothing happens.

Then I hold up the spoon, ignoring the curious looks they all give me, but the result is the same.

I dump it all back in my bag, about to give up, when I see the No Fishing sign Albie gave me. I remember how many people back home once believed in me. How, whether they know it or not, they're all counting on me to return their world to abnormal again.

Which means this is no time to stop believing in myself.

I stare hard at the jumbled bits of bones before me, and, from seemingly out of nowhere, a beautifully ornate golden frame begins to take shape. A frame that definitely wasn't there a moment ago, and isn't actually there now, or at least, not outside my head.

Just after that, the bones start to vibrate, as though

begging me to touch them, manipulate them, move them from their original positions into new ones that make sense.

Tentatively, I reach toward a phalange, trying not to cringe when I pinch it between my fingers. It's cold, a little slippery, but surprisingly sturdy considering how slender and fragile it is. In my head, I see it placed in the center of the frame, so that's where I move it on the canvas before me. Then I do the same for the ulnas and sternums, the humerus and clavicle. Urged on by the fever dream unspooling in my head, I rearrange the bones until the canvas seems to melt and swirl before me, taking on vibrant colors and patterns that form into shapes I can recognize.

I draw in a long, measured breath and steady myself before the masterpiece of bones. I'm hardly able to believe what has happened—that I'm actually seeing what I'm seeing—and the undeniable gravity of what it all means.

Is it possible that the price of magic is that I myself am becoming magical?

And with that in mind, was it really a warning at all?

I stare at the wondrous scene unfolding before me in a flurry of colors that light up the room.

And there, in the bottom right-hand corner, just as I expected, I see the name: *Penelope Ruggles.* Written in her usual fancy script.

The parting gift she left to me just before I started this journey.

Finally, after all these years, I'm on the receiving end of one of Penelope's pictures. And while it feels like a long time coming, as it turns out, it was right on time.

"Come on," I say, taking one last look at the image and committing it to memory. I turn on my heel and race toward the door. "We need to go, now!"

"Where to?" Frankie stares between the bone canvas and me.

"To Quiver Hollows," I tell her. Then, looking at Wolfhart, I say, "And you're driving."

THIRTY-SIX

BREAKING AND EXITING

We exit the bone palace, leaving everything in place since the bones we need are in the lab. After locating the truck, Wolfhart backs it up to the big double doors of the lab.

"They're locked," Fogbottom says. "What now?"

I'm about to try the spoon again when Wolfhart guns the engine, and shouts, "Everyone stand back! Don't make me say it twice!"

Before anyone can stop him, he's ramming the back of the truck through the doors.

Fogbottom cringes, Frankie watches wide-eyed, and I

look all around, wondering how many people he just woke from their beds thanks to the horrible, loud, crunching sound.

Three good rams are all it takes to make the doors splinter, cave, and bow in submission beneath the bed of the truck, leaving the lab cracked wide open.

"Told you driving was easy!" Wolfhart glances over his shoulder, an extra-wide grin planted across his face.

We need to get moving. With daylight already breaking, casting everything in varying shades of violet and blue, it won't be long before the other students begin waking. Well, the ones who aren't already awake, that is. And while we could certainly use the help to load all the bone dust, I'm not sure how many of these students we can trust. Some of them probably don't know anything else, and may not be open to change. People have a way of resisting anything that leads to uncertainty, even when something far better is waiting in the wings.

"Just start hauling everything into the bed of the truck," I say. "As much as you can get—as much as we can make fit."

Working as a team, we begin grasping, rolling, and loading the barrels. The truck is about three-quarters full when Frankie asks, "What is that?"

I follow the direction she's pointing. "Fresh kill," says Wolfhart.

Fogbottom winces, shaking his head. I blink and stare,

trying to make sense of the bleached heap of bones piled high on the table, ready for sorting.

"They're freshly boiled," Wolfhart continues. "About to be ground."

He speaks so matter-of-factly I can't help but wonder if he truly understands what it is that he's saying.

"It's disgusting, I know." Wolfhart looks at me. "But while these can't be saved, there are others that can. That's what we should focus on."

We load up the remaining barrels; then Wolfhart leads us to a small abandoned structure off to the side of the lab.

"It's the old guardhouse," Frankie explains. "Back when this used to be a prison." Then, looking at me, she says, "A prison is a place where they—"

"I know what a prison is," I tell her. "I've read a few books, you know."

We follow Wolfhart inside to where Moonsliver has hidden a bunch of small, frightened baby bunnies. A quick count tells me there are at least fifteen, possibly even twenty, but their cages are so small and they're so tightly crammed together that it's hard to say for sure.

"It's inhumane!" Frankie's cheeks flush with anger. "They look like they're barely hanging on."

Without a word, Fogbottom rips off his navy blazer, opens the cages, and starts grabbing armfuls of bunnies, which he then bundles into the soft lining of his jacket. A moment later, we follow his example. We've just made it back to the truck when a group of kids start streaming out of the building, their faces sleepy and bewildered as they try to make sense of such a dramatic change in their morning routine.

"What's going on?" A girl with a long blond ponytail steps forward.

Wolfhart ignores her, climbs inside the truck, and starts gunning the engine. *"Letsgoletsgoletsgoletsgo!"* he sings as Fogbottom squeezes into the backseat. I motion for Frankie to get in along with him.

But Frankie remains before me, shaking her head.

"Frankie—" I start, glancing nervously between the kids and her, wondering what she could possibly be up to. "We need to move, now!" I do my best to convince her, but Frankie stands firm.

"Someone needs to stay behind and look after them." Her face is solemn, her voice resigned.

"Frankie—no . . . ," I start, but the look in her eyes tells me it's futile to fight. No matter how hard I might try to convince her, her mind is made up.

"But—Quiver Hollows is your dream," I say, knowing it won't work, but refusing to give up so easily. "You said so yourself!"

"Go." She pushes a hand against my chest. "Go home. Do what you need to do. I'll be fine. I always am, aren't I?"

Wolfhart guns the engine again. "I'll leave without you—I swear I will!"

Taking him at his word, I shoot Frankie one last pleading look. Realizing this is the last time I'll ever see her, I pull the enchanted scroll from my bag and give it to her.

"This old broken thing?" She grins, exposing her slightly crooked front tooth.

"It works when it needs to," I say. "Turns out I had another piece of magic lined up. But who knows, maybe it will work for you if you ever find that you need it. If nothing else, I hope it will remind you to keep believing in magic, and to never lose faith in yourself."

She tucks the paper into her waistband and gives me another good hard shove toward the truck.

"Get the heck out of here, Grimsly Summerfield," she says. "Go keep the bones, or whatever you Keepers do."

I've barely so much as fastened my seat belt when Wolfhart flattens the pedal to the floor and crashes right through the front gate and onto the road.

THIRTY-SEVEN

MOONSLIVER LANDING

The truck lumbers down a long dirt road, sending gravel spitting and flying in all directions. Wolfhart alternately laughs and slaps the steering wheel, clearly enjoying himself, while Fogbottom and I desperately try to calm the bunnies and plead with him to slow down.

"Not a chance," Wolfhart shouts. "We can't let 'em catch us!"

I peer in the rearview mirror. "There's no one after us."

"That doesn't mean there won't be."

At least he's willing to follow directions. So when I tell

him to make a tight left at the first turnoff just ahead, he cranks the wheel hard, momentarily tipping the truck onto the rims of the two left wheels. Then it rights itself again and barrels down a road so narrow the sides scrape against a line of sturdy trees.

With the memory of Penelope's vision engraved in my brain, I continue directing him. The road grows increasingly bumpy and the visibility dim, forcing Wolfhart to ease up on the gas until we're barely coasting.

"What the heck?" Wolfhart leans forward until his forehead is practically pressed against the windshield.

"What is all that?" Fogbottom echoes, tentatively lowering his window. "This fog—it just came out of nowhere!"

I stare into the shroud of haze shimmering before us. It reminds me of the holographic show Frankie and I watched in the hole. And yet it's so strange to see it in person. I've never seen Quiver Hollows from the outside.

According to legend, those who dare to venture into the perpetual dome of fog, clouds, and mist usually end up panicked and lost, until they find their way back to where they started.

But now, thanks to the Moonslivers, the veil has thinned to the point where anyone wandering by could easily find their way inside.

"This is it," I tell them. "This is home." I'm forced to push the words past the lump that's formed in my throat. I spent only two days at the Seer's and four days in the academy, but I can already guess just how much has changed in my absence.

Still, knowing a word of warning is needed, I say, "Listen, I have no idea what we'll find, but you need to know that Quiver Hollows is not a normal place. In fact, it's the exact opposite of normal, or rather, it used to be, but anyway." I shake my head and start again. "You might see the sort of things or the kinds of people that defy explanation. Things you're not used to seeing outside of movies or books. But it's real, not the result of special effects. Every single thing you see in this place is one hundred percent authentic. So if it turns out that it's too weird for you, or if you're freaked out being around people who look nothing like you, then it's probably better to just stop now and let me take it from here."

I eyeball each of them and receive two blank looks in return.

"I'm serious," I say. "People here may look odd, but they're good people. The best people. And if you even so much as try to bully them, so help me I'll—"

Before I can finish, Wolfhart is lowering his window and saying, "Is that girl a mermaid?"

I squint into the distance. A girl with peeling blue and green scales on her legs pauses on a corner, nervously looking both ways before darting across the road and disappearing behind a grove of trees.

"Not exactly," I say. "But it's a good example of the sort of thing you'll encounter."

"Then count me in!"

Wolfhart revs the engine as Fogbottom says, "What are we waiting for? No way am I missing out on this!"

Next thing I know, the truck is back to bumping along the road. "Make a right up ahead," I say, figuring we'll drive through the center of town on our way to Summerfield Lawn. It's the fastest route for us to restore the bones and set things right once again.

Wolfhart and Fogbottom are mesmerized by the view that unfolds outside their windows. In a way I am too, only for entirely different reasons.

The storefronts are all shuttered and closed. It's just after dawn, so logically, I guess that could explain it. Except for the fact that the majority of the windows are also broken, with big mounds of glass glittering on the sidewalks and streets. There are also really offensive slurs scrolled on the sides of the buildings that definitely weren't there before. Stuff like:

Down with scales!

Manifesters are crooks!

Tails are for losers!

Spoon benders are liars and fakes!

"Was it always like this?" Wolfhart steers around a burning trash can set smack in the middle of the street.

"No," I whisper. "Not even close."

While the streets aren't exactly desolate, the few people who are roaming about appear haggard, desperate, and lost—as abandoned and discarded as the storefronts.

When we pass the town center, and I see that the statue of Yegor Quiver has been replaced with twin effigies of Vitaly and Boris Moonsliver, along with a large sign that reads:

WELCOME TO MOONSLIVER LANDING!
A NON-MAGICAL PLACE, EST. 2017

I can't help but wonder if maybe I got here too late.

"Hurry," I say, hunkering down in my seat. "We need to get to Summerfield Lawn, and quickly. There's no time to waste."

THIRTY-EIGHT

MAGIC TREE HOUSE

"Stop!" I throw my door open and jump before Wolfhart even has a chance to hit the brake.

With my bag flapping against my chest, I sprint across the lawn—a lawn that has now turned as dead and brown as the one at Moonsliver Academy—and pause before the tall, thick metal wall surrounding the property.

To be fair, I knew about Snelling's wall. Ming, Penelope, and Ollie told me about it just before I left for the outside world. Still, it's one thing to hear about it and quite another to see it up close and in person.

I crane my neck and follow the line of metal all the way to the top, figuring it must span at least three stories, possibly more. But what really strikes me is that there's no gate to be found. No way in, no way out. Which means Snelling is in there, somewhere, cut off from the rest of the world.

I walk the perimeter only to confirm that it's true. Not knowing what else to do, I call his name. "Snelling— Snelling!" I repeatedly shout. But the metal is so thick my voice just boomerangs right back.

Unfortunately, the wall extends all the way around Summerfield Lawn as well, which means without Snelling's help, I have no way of returning the bones, no way to right all these wrongs.

Unless . . .

I race back to the truck and direct Wolfhart to turn around and drive toward the very edge of the forest.

"There's a forest?" His voice is as incredulous as his face.

I look beyond the windshield and see what he sees: big walls, dead grass, abandoned streets, and no shortage of derogatory graffiti. It's urban blight at its worst, which makes the idea of a nearby forest seem improbable at best.

"I guess we'll see," I say. I'm no longer certain of anything.

He noses the truck down the path. Sure enough, the trees that once grew charmingly crooked are now ramrod straight.

"This is it," I tell him. "Leave the truck. We'll walk the rest of the way."

"But what about the bone dust? And the bunnies?"

I take a moment to consider. "Leave the bone dust, bring the bunnies. We'll hang out here until I decide what to do."

With each of us carrying a bundle of bunnies, we trudge toward the fort.

"Where are we going?" Fogbottom says. "I don't see anything."

"That's the point," I tell him. Not bothering to explain how the point of the fort was to hide in plain sight. That it was crafted to blend into the landscape so well it's easy to miss.

"Can you at least tell us what we're looking for?" Wolfhart struggles to balance the squirming bundle of bunnies clutched in his arms. "And shouldn't we let these little guys out so they're free to frolic or hop or whatever it is bunnies do?"

"Not yet," I say, unwilling to make a move until I have a better feel for what we've gotten ourselves into.

We head deeper into a thick grove of trees. I remember how the ground beneath my feet was once covered in a luxurious blanket of moss, but now it's dead and dried out, cracking and splintering in protest.

Yet there's still something really beautiful about the way the long fingers of sun poke through the branches and light up our path. Those lean slivers of light bouncing, refracting, and leaving everything shiny and dappled with promise. The sight of it serving as a sort of cruel reminder that if I am successful in turning things back to abnormal, then the dome of fog, clouds, and mist will return, making a moment like this completely unthinkable.

The sun isn't our friend. I repeat the phrase in my head. It's the work of the Moonslivers. And while it may look pretty on the surface and feel nice and warm against my skin, the fact that it's even able to break through in the first place only shows just how vulnerable Quiver Hollows has become.

I guess the lack of sunshine is the price we pay to keep the magic alive.

Magic always comes with a price.

"Just up ahead!" I shake away the thoughts and quicken my pace as the others jog alongside me.

"Where?" Wolfhart looks around. "I don't see anything."

"Me either," Fogbottom echoes. "Not a thing."

"I meant that literally," I say. "Look up. It's a tree fort."

My gaze roams the length of the tree. Now that the trunk has straightened, the fort is much higher than it used to be. It also hangs at a really odd angle.

"What's that?" Wolfhart points.

I follow the length of his extended finger to see Ming looping down from the branches.

"Grimsly?" She blinks rapidly, as though she doesn't quite trust what she sees. "What happened to all your hair?"

I run a hand self-consciously over my scalp and determine it's not worth explaining.

I hug her. Quickly, briefly, mostly surprised that she lets me. A sure sign that things are even worse than I thought. Ming isn't normally the hugging type. After I introduce her to Fogbottom and Wolfhart, Ming settles before me and I see how tired and weary she looks. Her face is pale, her bangs hang limp against her forehead, and her feathered dress has lost all its flutter.

"What took you so long?" Her narrowed gaze darts between us. "And what's with the bunnies?"

"Long story short, we found them in the outside world."

"They probably ran away." Her voice is muted, her dark eyes rimmed with fatigue. "Well, good for them. I'd run away too if I had anywhere to go. The magic's all gone. Everyone's turning against each other . . ." She pauses as though there's more, but then she dismisses it with a wave of her hand. "Anyway, come on." She makes for the ladder, which takes me by surprise. Sensing the question I haven't yet asked, she says, "All the magic really is gone. I can't levitate anymore."

And just like *that*, my heart breaks in half.

At the door of the fort, she knocks three times in quick succession, followed by two knocks, followed by a single short whistle. The secret code required for entrance that we made up long ago, way back before there was even a need for a secret code.

A moment later, Ming pushes the door open and ushers us all quickly inside, then pulls the door shut.

I blink into the darkness, needing a moment for my eyes to adjust before I can see Penelope huddled in the corner with a blanket pulled tightly around her shoulders.

"What's wrong with her?" I hesitate to go any further.

"She's haunted," Ming says, her face grave. "Only she's haunted by visions, not ghosts."

I study Penelope. Her eyes are shut tight as she rocks back and forth, mumbling a string of indecipherable words to herself.

"Remember how she had that vision of you failing the spoon-bending exam?"

I nod. I remember it all too well.

"Well, that was the first time she ever experienced such a thing. As it turns out, it wasn't the last. She's been having lots of visions over the last few days, ever since you left, and according to her, each one is worse than the last. It's like living a constant nightmare," Ming says. "A nightmare that refuses to end."

I kneel beside Penelope and rest a hand on her shoulder. After calling her name a few times to no avail, I do the only thing I can think of: I place a bundle of bunnies before her, hoping it might make her feel better. Then I stand back and watch as she scoops them into her arms and cradles a few to her cheek.

"Thanks," I whisper.

She shoots me a questioning look.

"Your parting gift. The picture—it helped more than you know."

She closes her eyes and retreats back into her world, but I know she heard me, or at least I think she did.

"Where's Ollie?" I look around.

Ming sighs, tells us to sit, then catches us up on everything that's happened since I left. It pretty much amounts to what I already know just from driving around. Walls have been built. Neighbors are at war. Those with tails, scales, and the ability to bend spoons have all turned on each other. The Moonslivers have completely taken over.

"They took Ollie," she says, her voice sullen. "He's a spoon bender and a Quiver, and they're determined to make him pay."

"And Snelling?" I ask, almost afraid to hear the answer.

"They took him as well." She looks down at the ground. "No one has seen either of them. They're trapped somewhere inside the wall Snelling built."

"How can they be trapped?" I ask. This doesn't make any sense. "Ollie and Snelling are the best benders around—surely they can find a way to break out! Especially if it's a wall Snelling built."

"Like I said, the magic is gone, Grimsly." Ming's face is unbearably sad. "I can't levitate, Ollie can't bend, and

Penelope's haunted. We're useless. Now I know what you must've felt like all of these years." Then, as if realizing what she just said, she slaps a hand over her mouth and tries to backtrack. "I didn't mean . . . What I meant to say was . . ."

I wave it away. I don't have time for hurt feelings. Besides, it's not like it isn't true. I did feel useless back then, but I don't anymore.

I scramble to my feet and motion for Wolfhart and Fogbottom to follow. "We're going back to Snelling's," I tell them. "And no matter what it takes, this time we'll find a way in."

We race for the door, when Penelope calls from the corner. "Grimsly?" she says.

I turn to look at her.

She closes her eyes as though trying to transmit a picture. When nothing comes through, she shakes her head sadly and whispers, "Hurry."

THIRTY-NINE

BONE EATERS

"What'd you see?" Ming slides into the backseat of the truck alongside Fogbottom as I climb up front next to Wolfhart.

There was a time, not so long ago, when that question would've thrilled me. The thought that Ming would think Penelope could transmit a picture that I could actually see would've made me feel, well, like I belonged in this place.

But the fact is, I didn't see anything. Then again, I didn't need to. The sadness of Penelope's gaze told me everything I need to know.

"What is it the Moonslivers want?" Ming asks. "I don't understand any of this."

"They want to rid Quiver Hollows of all its magic," Fog-bottom says. Then, looking at me, he adds, "Well, that's the gist, right?"

I nod, my focus trained on the view beyond the windshield.

"But why?" Ming glances between all three of us.

I take my time before answering. I could say it's because he wants revenge, or because he wants to reverse a curse that his ancestor unwittingly brought on him; both of those statements are true. But it also goes deeper than that. The question is more complicated than it may seem on the surface.

So instead I say, "Because a long time ago, Vitaly Moonsliver dared to believe in magic and love. And when he lost the person he loved most, he blamed this place and its magic. He lashed out at everyone around him and at Quiver Hollows in general. By doing so, not only was he physically ejected from town and sent back to the outside world, but his words ended up putting a curse on his family for every generation to come."

"And how exactly is that our fault?" Ming makes an outraged face.

"It isn't," I tell her. "But Moonsliver doesn't see it that way. It's always easier to play the victim than to take responsibility.

Moonsliver spent the first part of his life debunking magic, and the one time he dared to open his heart and believe in it, his heart broke wide open. So he shoved all the shattered pieces back together and refused to ever believe in anything again."

"You make it sound . . . sort of romantic," Ming says.

"I don't mean to. As you can see, the consequences have been serious. Not only for many generations before us, but for more still to come." I stop there, not quite ready to confess that I'm part of that long chain of Moonslivers, which means someday the curse will be true for me too.

Unless I can find a way to break it without breaking the town along with it.

In the silence, Fogbottom adds, "They think that by destroying the magic in this place, they can destroy the curse. They won't be happy until the people are broken and the earth is left scorched."

"The people *are* broken," I say, thinking of Penelope, the girl with the peeling scales and frightened gaze, along with all the townspeople who are so blinded by fear they built walls to shut each other out.

"Not all of 'em," Ming says. "Not us."

"Not us," I agree.

At my instruction, Wolfhart drives around the entire perimeter of the property as we search for a way in.

"I don't get it." I frown. "If Snelling built the wall before the Moonslivers got here, then how did the Moonslivers get in? There must be a way to enter and exit."

"Did you see one?" Fogbottom asks.

I shake my head.

"Maybe they dug a hole," Wolfhart says. "Maybe they tunneled their way in."

"It's possible," I say.

"Except we can't be sure that the Moonslivers are actually in there," Ming says as we all turn to look at her. "Just because they're holding Snelling and Ollie captive doesn't mean they're in there with them."

"But then how did Ollie get in?" I ask. "Snelling built the wall before Ollie was in there. You're sure they're in there?"

Ming sighs. "Rumor has it. Although I guess I'm not sure of anything anymore. I haven't seen a sign of him anywhere else, and I know the Moonslivers were after him for being a descendant of the Quivers."

"So it's a mystery." Wolfhart studies the wall. "No way in, no way out, except that there is. There always is. Anyway, where do we start?" He pulls the truck to the front of Snelling's property.

"As the Keeper, I need to return the bones to Summerfield Lawn."

"Except you can't access Summerfield Lawn," Ming says.

"Never mind the fact that the bones are no longer bones," Fogbottom reminds me.

Ming looks at me in confusion and I take a moment to explain how the bones have been ground into dust.

"So how will you know which bits go where?" she asks.

"I'm not sure it matters," Wolfhart starts. Ming immediately whirls on him, and he raises his hands in defense. "What I mean is, it's impossible to separate them. There's clearly no way to do that. But here's the thing: Bone dust, or rather bone meal, is often used as fertilizer for soil and plants and as food supplements for animals. It can be controversial, and some people claim it leads to disease. But since these animals are, or rather *were* magical, then don't you think that maybe the same principles apply here? I mean, if you really are the Keeper, well, you still have the bones, just in a different form. So if you sprinkle the dust around, not just in the graves but all around the town, maybe it will restore the magic."

"For someone not raised on magic, you sure have caught on quickly." Ming studies him so intently Wolfhart's face reddens under her gaze.

"In my life before the academy, before I lost my whole family, I lived on a farm," he tells her.

"I'm sorry," Ming says.

Wolfhart nods. The rest of us sit in silence.

"Maybe we can even feed some to the bunnies," Fogbottom pipes up, eliciting a sharp scowl from Ming.

"No. No way. That's disgusting," she says.

"Is it?" Wolfhart asks, and after thinking about it for a bit, Ming shrugs.

"Actually," I say, "we're going to take it a step further than that."

I look at Ming, remembering how sneaking the bone dust worked to help Frankie soar out the roof of the hole and aid our escape. Maybe, if it gave Frankie a touch of magic, it can restore the magic that's currently lying dormant in my friend.

"You're going to eat it," I tell her. Before she can protest, I add, "And after that you're going to levitate right over this wall and help us find a way in so we can deal with the Moonslivers once and for all."

FORTY

FLYING MING

We roll a barrel out of the bed of the truck and pry the lid open.

"So, what?" Ming says. "I dip a finger in and lick it?"

"It might take a bit more than that," I tell her.

Reluctantly, she cups her hands together, scoops them inside the barrel, and fills them with bone dust. She stares at the mound of ivory-colored powder for a moment. Then, with an exaggerated grimace, she shuts her eyes and funnels it straight down her throat.

"How do you feel?" I study her closely.

Wolfhart leans closer. "What does it taste like?"

Ming swallows, swipes a hand across her mouth. "I feel thirsty. As for the taste . . ." She takes a moment to consider. "It tastes just like chicken." She laughs.

"So what do you think?" I point at the wall.

"I think that's really high." She speaks with so much trepidation it takes me by surprise. I've known Ming all my life and I can't recall a single moment where she's ever doubted herself. It's awful to see her brought to this point.

"You've gone higher," I remind her. "Way higher. Lots of times."

She rubs her lips together as though trying to envision such a thing, but her gaze remains unconvinced as Wolfhart and Fogbottom wait to see something cool happen.

Ming straightens her spine and jumps in place as though warming up for a race.

After a moment, she says, "Here goes nothing, or everything." Then, without another word, she spots her destination, gets her feet into position, and leaps toward the top of the high metal wall.

"Whoa!" Fogbottom cries, staring in disbelief at the sight of Ming flying high above our heads.

"Dude, seriously? That is sick!" Wolfhart echoes.

And though I've seen it a million times before, I can't hide the excitement from my voice when I say, "Ming's not just levitating, she's actually *flying!*"

"Um, guys." She soars in a series of wide circles around the property. "This is really cool and all, but I'm not sure I know how to land!"

"Aim for a tree!" Fogbottom shouts.

"Are you crazy?" Wolfhart cries. "Do you see how fast she's going? She could easily crash and impale herself on one of the branches!"

"What—you have a better idea?" Fogbottom says.

"Breathe," I tell her. "Spot your landing, and come down slowly and gently. You've got this—you've—"

Ming drops out of sight, and we wait in tense silence until we hear her muffled voice from the other side of the wall.

The sound is garbled, distorted by the thick metal. Though it sounds something like: "Grimsly, I can't find an entrance. I can see Moonsliver in the upstairs window!"

FORTY-ONE

THE POWER WITHIN

"Now what?" Fogbottom asks.

I stand before the wall. I have no idea.

"I mean, it's so thick," Fogbottom says. "We need, like—a giant can opener or something to break in there."

"A can opener? Really?" Wolfhart rolls his eyes and shakes his head.

"This is Snelling's work," I say to no one in particular, trying to organize all the thoughts in my head. "And since Snelling's the master, I'm not sure it's even possible to break through. Not unless he wants you to, which he clearly didn't. That was the point of building this."

"But if Moonsliver is in there like Ming says, then there's a way. There has to be an opening somewhere."

Ming completes yet another surveillance of the property, only to confirm what I'm thinking.

"There's no break in the wall." She lands before me. "Though there could be a tunnel. I can keep looking."

"Why don't I ram the truck right into it, like I ran it into the lab and the front gate at school?"

"Won't work," I tell him. "It'll only mess up the truck, which I need you to use for something else."

He looks at me. "Just say the word."

And while I'm less sure it's loyalty toward me than an attempt to impress Ming, I'll take what I can get.

"That was a good idea you had about sprinkling the bone dust all over town."

His face lights up a thousand watts.

"So I want you and Fogbottom to use the truck and do exactly that. You drive while Fogbottom sprinkles."

"I sprinkle?" Fogbottom glares. "Why do I have to sprinkle? Why can't I drive?"

"Seriously?" Ming steps before him. "Are we seriously going to do this?"

Just like that, Fogbottom shakes his head and backs down. Ming nods for me to continue.

"You'll roll a barrel toward the edge of the bed and slowly release the bone dust. Concentrate on the area around town and, well, just get as much of the place as you can. And remember, a little goes a long way. Also, don't use all the barrels. Save one to sprinkle here."

They look at me.

"Actually, save two. One for Summerfield Lawn and one for . . . well, to be determined."

"That still doesn't answer how we're going to breach the wall," Ming reminds me.

"I have an idea." I scoop my hands into the bone dust and funnel it into my mouth just like Ming did a few moments ago. I'm not even sure why, since it's not like there's any real magic lying dormant within me. The only magic I've been able to work so far has come from some other source, like the enchanted scroll, or the picture Penelope sent me. But I figure since I'm the Keeper, maybe it will help me to fulfill my duty. It's worth a try.

Aware of everyone staring at me, I lick my lips and say, "She's right, it tastes just like chicken."

After a moment Wolfhart asks, "What if we try eating some of that?"

He gestures toward the barrel, and my first instinct is to say no. It's too risky. There's no way of knowing what the results will be or how it might go.

But then, I think: What if the magic it gives is the magic you already had inside of you?

For instance, the Moonslivers both ate it, and it's not like they're suddenly flying around or bending metal (at least, not that I know of). It merely allowed them to access Quiver Hollows—something that a Moonsliver from long ago was already capable of doing, thanks to a little help from Yegor Quiver—but still. And for all I know, it helped them penetrate the wall as well.

Finally, I nod at Wolfhart. "Sure," I say. "Why not? What could it hurt?" I watch as he fills his hands with powder, and Fogbottom soon follows suit. Then they funnel it into their mouths.

"Ready?" I ask.

Wolfhart jangles the keys as Fogbottom climbs into the back of the truck. And then they're off, leaving a trail of bone dust in their path.

"So what's the plan?" Ming asks, watching them go.

"Once again, you're going to leap high into the sky," I say. "Only this time, you're taking me with you."

FORTY-TWO

BIRD ENVY

Flying is not overrated.

Not even close.

The feeling of soaring through the air, weightless, and temporarily immune to the pull of gravity, well, it makes me feel insanely jealous of every single bird fortunate enough to take that experience for granted.

But just like the old saying goes: what goes up must come down.

We land with a thud near the backside of the house. I get to my feet, brush myself off, and struggle to take in the scene before me, but it's impossible to process in a single glance.

It's also impossible to process in several more glances, but I do what I can.

My gaze travels the path that leads to Summerfield Lawn before it wends its way back around to where I now stand.

I guess I thought it would be easy.

Somehow I thought our biggest challenge, our only real challenge, would be to get past the wall.

Once that was done, I figured we'd storm in and . . .

And act like a bunch of heroes, I suppose.

But now, with Summerfield Lawn left scorched by what looks to have been a raging fire, one that left the long rows of memorials melted and mangled into an oversized blob, it's clear that I'm in over my head.

I mean, yeah, I'm the Keeper. And even though I never received a full definition of what that means, I've deduced that it's my responsibility to keep the bones where they belong. I protect the binding magic of the town, which is kind of a big deal. A big deal that I admittedly flubbed.

But now, even though I'm set to return the bones, or rather, the bone dust, it's clear the job doesn't end there.

I'm being called to do something way beyond the line of duty, and with so much at stake, I can't afford to fail the way I did the last time I stood in this spot.

"Grimsly? You okay?" Ming places a cautious hand on my shoulder.

I fiddle nervously with the strap on my bag. I'm not sure how to answer. I'm not up for lying and claiming I've got it all under control when that couldn't be further from the truth.

"What should we do?" she whispers.

"I have no idea what will happen next," I tell her.

"So . . . we're winging it?" Her brow rises so high it disappears beneath her bangs.

I nod.

"Grimsly?"

I look at her.

"You said there were two Moonslivers, and I'm pretty sure I only saw one."

"We'll find 'em both," I say. "Not to worry."

I reach for the door, and my hand instinctively recoils when the slightest touch sends it gaping wide open.

Ming and I exchange a worried look.

"That's creepy," she whispers.

"Which window did you see him in?"

"Upstairs . . ." She takes a moment to think. "Your bedroom."

"You sure?" I press for details, wanting to make sure before we reach the landing at the top of the stairs and head the wrong way. Every move is important. Quiver Hollows's future is at stake.

This time when she nods, she does so with conviction. "You have those filmy curtains. You know, with the stars and moon pattern. I could see a man silhouetted just on the other side of them."

As a little kid, I was obsessed with the moon and stars. Growing up in Quiver Hollows, we were told of their existence, but because of the perpetual dome of fog, clouds, and mist we were never able to see them. I guess the idea of a solar system and planets and galaxies and constellations became so mythical to me that at one point my entire room was decorated in an astronomical theme. Eventually I got rid of it all, but I hung on to the curtains. I liked to watch the way the fabric glowed when I got ready for bed—the way the moon and stars shone against the darkness of night made me feel like I was looking at the real thing.

Funny to think how I was just in the outside world and yet I never looked up long enough to appreciate all the magic in the sky. I wonder if it's the same for people who live in the outside world full-time. I wonder if they're so used to the miracle unfolding every night that they stop noticing its existence.

Ming starts to float up the stairs, but I tug on the back of her dress to stop her.

"Moonsliver's big and mean," I say. "I think I should go first."

"Because I'm a girl?" She narrows her eyes and hitches the side of her mouth.

"No, because you can fly. So while he's looking at me at eye level, you can catch him off guard."

She takes a moment to consider. "Fine," she agrees. "But maybe we should both take one of these to defend ourselves."

She grabs a couple fire pokers from the hearth and hands one to me. Then, slowly, carefully, I make my way up the stairs as Ming flutters behind.

At the top of the landing I press my back to the wall and creep down the hallway. When I'm just shy of the entry, I signal for her to wait. Then I throw open the door and gasp in surprise when I see Moonsliver looming with a giant ax in his hand.

FORTY-THREE

MISTAKEN IDENTITY

Most people, when confronted by an ax-wielding fiend, would probably run the opposite way.

Me, I rush straight toward it.

Moving quickly, I'm counting on the element of surprise to work in my favor and keep me from getting hacked to bits.

Only it doesn't work.

Moonsliver launches right at me.

In the dim room, he appears massive, even bigger and broader than I remember him being. With his ax gripped firmly in his fist, he is imposing, threatening, completely un-defeatable.

I close my eyes and swing wildly. Fueled by a surge of adrenaline-laced fear, I'm several swings in before I realize Moonsliver's not fighting back.

In fact, he hasn't made a single effort to defend himself.

I watch in confusion as he wobbles precariously, staggers backward, and crashes hard against the wall.

His head detaches, hits the floor hard, and rolls away from his neck while his body continues to judder and jerk, eliciting a loud and horrible clang that rings through my ears and jangles my bones.

I stare uncertainly, needing a moment so that my thoughts can catch up to what my gut already knows.

It's not Moonsliver.

It's not even human.

It's the statue of Yegor Quiver that once stood in the center of town.

He's draped in a navy blazer and white shirt, and the bent spoon he once struck toward the sky has been replaced with an ax. But there's no mistaking that it's Yegor, not Head-master Moonsliver.

My hand fumbles across the wall. Locating the light switch, I kneel closer to get a better look.

The statue was on wheels. That's how it came at me. The Moonslivers rigged this whole room. They tricked me.

Lured me here and purposely staged it this way so that, for a few moments, anyway, I would believe it was Vitaly.

The Moonslivers set the trap, and I strolled right in.

And then I remember—*Ming!*

I call her name, spin in circles, thinking maybe she got scared and went to hide somewhere. But Ming doesn't scare easily, and she certainly never hides.

I race into the hallway and look around, but there's no sign of her.

Or at least, that's what I think, until I spot a single pink feather lying on the ground at the top of the stairs.

A few stairs down, there's another.

I follow the trail of feathers all the way out the back door and across the scorched land leading to Summerfield Lawn, where Boris and Vitaly are waiting.

FORTY-FOUR

BONE CRUSHER

I'm alone.

It's the first thing that pops into my head, even though technically, it's not really true.

The Moonslivers are here. And someplace, somewhere, I'm guessing Ming, Ollie, and Snelling are too. Also, somewhere on the other side of the wall, Wolfhart and Fogbottom are hard at work, restoring the magic to Quiver Hollows.

Or at least, I hope that's what they're doing.

No way to know for sure, or if it'll work.

All of which brings me right back to my original thought: I really am alone.

Me versus the Moonslivers.

I adjust the strap on my bag and square my gaze on each of them.

"So it looks like I was right." Vitaly nods at me, then smirks at Boris. "Boris swore you'd never find your way out of the hole. But I told him you're far more resourceful than you look."

"What do you want?" I eyeball each of them.

"At the moment, not much. It would appear I have everything I ever needed, no?"

"You sure about that?" I speak with just enough edge to fill Vitaly with doubt. It only lasts a second, but the flash of hesitation in his eyes gives me something to cling to. "I mean, there's still the matter of the curse."

"How did you—" Boris lunges toward me in anger, but before he can go any further, Vitaly thrusts an arm out to stop him.

"Isn't that what this is all about?" I wave a hand. "Reversing the curse that's haunted your family for generations?"

Your family.

My family.

One and the same.

But they don't need to know that.

Not yet.

Not ever, if I can help it.

"I don't know what you're talking about." Vitaly narrows his eyes.

"I think you do." I hold my ground.

"You know what I think?" Boris asks. "I think the more you insist on talking, the closer your friends come to dying."

My gaze darts between them. Are they father and son? Grandfather and grandson? It's impossible to tell. I know Boris is around my age, but Vitaly is like Snelling; he's in a sort of indefinable category. None of which matters at the moment. Funny what an overstressed mind will come up with to distract itself.

"Where are they?" I say. "What have you done with them?"

"Well, as much as we've grown fond of the bone dust—the bulk of it coming from those colorful bunnies and what we managed to recover from the graves—we're thinking if there's that much power in animal bones, just think of the power that might be found in human bones."

"Humans like your ancestors?" I snap.

They look at me as though they don't understand.

"Memento mori," I remind them. "I saw your creepy crypt keepers' room. I guess that's one way to memorialize your fallen family members."

"You went into *the room*?" Vitaly's eyes blaze. His body begins to shake with rage. It reminds me of the holographic Vitaly.

"Of course." I do my best to keep him occupied with the breach as my gaze darts discreetly. I'm on the lookout for some sign of my friends, a hint as to where the Moonslivers might be keeping them.

"That room is sacred. You had no right to go in there!"

"And you had no right to return here," I tell him. "And yet here we are, having violated each other's space. So what happens now?"

Moonsliver's nostrils flatten and flare as his face becomes so enraged, so inflamed, it morphs from its usual shade of tomato to a shocking shade of ripe tangerine.

"You watch your friends die!" His voice thunders. "You watch your town lose every last trace of its magic. Then it's mine to control."

"And then what?" I say.

He looks at me curiously.

"You control the town, and then what? You open another academy? You become the mayor of Moonsliver Landing?" I pause like I have all the time in the world.

"All that and more!" Boris boasts.

"But you'll still be under the curse." I shrug. "So really, what's the point? All those motherless Moonslivers ... Seems so sad, when you think about it."

"The curse will be reversed," Vitaly says. "Once the magic is gone, then—"

Before he can finish, I say, "That's not how it works."

He stops talking and studies my face.

Pieces of what Frankie told me float through my mind. "In order to reverse the curse, you need a reversal spell."

Boris looks at Vitaly, but Vitaly is quick to say, "He's bluffing. Don't listen to him."

"Let my friends go, and I'll reverse the curse," I tell him.

Vitaly shakes his head firmly. He doesn't even allow a moment in which to consider. "No," he says. "Not a chance."

I start to speak again, refusing to give up quite so easily. Before I can begin, Vitaly steps forward, grabs me by the collar, and says, "I've had enough of your games. You want to know where your friends are?"

I swallow hard. Try to jerk free.

"They're right there. Hiding in plain sight."

He spins me around until I'm staring at what looks to be a large metal box.

"It's a bone crusher," Vitaly tells me, his voice a little too gleeful. "It's a recent invention, and I'm happy to report that it works very well. Much more efficient than the way we used to do it, which required all manner of grisly messiness I won't bother to explain. You see, the way this works is I flip the switch and a heavy metal plate descends, pressing down on everything in its path until it's crushed to bits. Then, after all the blood and organs and other liquidy, squishy parts are drained away, we put what remains through the grinder. And voilà! A barrel of bone dust made and several steps saved."

"Why do you need so much bone dust?" I ask. My eyes remain glued to the box. "What could you possibly be doing with all that?" I swallow hard and force myself to face him. "Nothing you do makes any sense! First you run a school that teaches that magic isn't real, then you use magic in your attempt to shut down the very place where magic is indisputably real, and then you stockpile all the magical bone dust. What's your endgame? Why are you doing all this?"

And then time slows down. Everything blurs except the space between Vitaly, Boris, and me.

"Magic is powerful," Vitaly says. "Far too powerful to be given so freely to those who waste it on things like rainbow lakes and blue bunnies. Those who control the magic control the world." He grins triumphantly.

"That's your plan?" I say. "To control the world?"

"Not the whole world," Vitaly says. "Or at least, not yet. For now, just our corner of it is enough. But who knows, maybe someday."

"There's still the matter of the curse," I tell him. "You can't get around that."

"There's also still the matter of your friends," he retorts, pointing at the box. "And you can't get around that either. Though I imagine it will be fun watching you try."

He gestures to Boris, who grins at me as he flips the switch.

A second later, earsplitting shrieks pierce the air as the crusher begins its descent and my friends scream in fear.

FORTY-FIVE

OUTSIDE THE BOX

Inside the box, my friends yell, scream, and pound on the sides, desperately trying to find a way out.

Outside the box, I stare stupidly, pathetically, wondering what I can possibly do to turn this around.

I still have no magical skills to speak of. My friends are the most magical people I know, but other than Ming, their powers have been stripped clean. And since Ming's only power is her ability to fly, it won't help under the circumstances.

"Make no mistake," Vitaly says, his voice competing with

the shrieking—both machine and human. "The plate is very heavy. Made of solid metal. And it's been perfectly calibrated to run from the top of the box to the bottom in five minutes flat. Oh, and only so you know, fifty-five seconds have already elapsed. Oops, make that fifty-six, fifty-seven . . . one minute down . . . well, you get the gist."

My fists clench uselessly as I look around, searching for some sort of loophole, someone on my side, anyone or anything who might be able to help. But it's just me and my cousin and my uncle—or whoever Vitaly is to me.

Wolfhart and Fogbottom are still out there. But even if returning the bone dust to the earth does work, there's no telling how long it will take to restore the magic.

"Two minutes gone." Vitaly shakes his head.

"Make that two minutes and fifteen seconds," Boris pipes up. "And counting," he adds with a laugh.

I really am alone.

The only person with no discernable power, left in charge of saving the ones I love most.

I close my eyes for a moment, forcing myself to dig deep and think—think of something I can do to stop this from happening.

I can try to overpower the Moonslivers . . . but there's no way that will work. I'm outnumbered. Vitaly is the size of a building. Boris is nastier than I assumed.

I can try to negotiate again with the promise of reversing

the curse. Except it didn't work at the start of this mess, so it definitely won't work now.

I open my eyes and gaze out at what remains of Summerfield Lawn—the place I once called my own—where I found a purpose, a way to be of service to others. My vision burns at the sight of it. My throat grows scratchy and tight. I'm *this* close to losing everything and everyone I care about most. The thought alone is enough to knock the breath right out of me.

Quiver Hollows is the only home I've ever known. The only home I ever want to know. Despite my being a Moonsliver, the townspeople welcomed me, accepted me, helped to raise me. They treated me as one of their own.

I'm the one who was so focused on our differences I convinced myself I didn't belong.

"Three minutes," Vitaly says. "Wow, you really are quite useless, aren't you?"

I let my people down. Unfortunately, I have no idea how to turn that around. Summerfield Lawn is so unrecognizable, I feel like I'm standing at the edge of the world.

The edge of the world . . .

When did I last feel that way?

The Seer.

I've watched this before.

It's part of my destiny.

Though how it will end remains a mystery.

"You've got a minute and a half left," Vitaly says. "Just to give you a visual, at this point, your friends—the ones who are still alive, anyway—are crouched as low on the floor as they can go. Notice how they've stopped screaming? That's because they've given up on you. They realize you're inept, unable to help them. Now they'll have to make their peace with surrendering their lives for the empowerment of the Moonslivers. At least they're dying for a good cause."

I grind my jaw and glare at Vitaly. "Not on my watch," I say.

I turn away from the Moonslivers and settle my focus squarely on the large metal box. Then, just like Snelling taught me, I envision the plate pausing, stopping, and reversing itself.

I envision it rising again as the sides of the box bend and curl like flower petals greeting the sun.

In my heart, I believe it's working.

In my bones, I know I can do this.

I'm better than my birthright, better than the Moonsliver blood that flows deep within me.

It's Snelling who raised me, Snelling who taught me I could do anything I set my mind to.

And right now, I'm setting my mind, totally, completely, and wholly, to blowing this box wide open.

"Thirty seconds," Boris calls. "And just so you know, if they're not flattened on their bellies like pancakes by now, it's too late to save them."

"Twenty-five," Vitaly sings gleefully.

I hold my focus, aware of the heat thrumming through me, causing my limbs to quiver, my bones to quake.

"Twenty . . . nineteen!" Boris breaks into giggles as he and Vitaly fist-bump to what they consider guaranteed victory.

"How does it feel to fail?" Boris taunts me. "How does it feel to disappoint everyone who counted on you? Huh, Gutter Rat? Do tell!"

Boris continues his mocking.

Vitaly triumphantly counts down the seconds.

But while they're busy taunting and celebrating and dancing around, they miss the fact that the groaning and shrieking has shifted into something else entirely. The plate is reversing itself and heading the opposite way.

While they're busy calling me names, they miss the fact that the sides of the box are now separating at the corners, splitting at the seams, and bending and curling and spooling toward the ground as my friends begin to rise wearily and look around.

"I think it's your turn to tell me what it feels like to fail." I glance between Vitaly and Boris. "I can hardly remember," I tell them. "It seems like so long ago now."

I nod toward the scene unfolding behind them, savoring the look on Vitaly's face transitioning from smug delight to absolute horror as he watches Snelling rise from the gnarled box of twisted metal.

FORTY-SIX

BAD BLOODLINES

"You never did know when to quit, did you?" Snelling towers over Moonsliver, his eyes as icy as I've ever seen them, the words flung from his tongue sharp and snarling. "You never get when it's time to surrender."

Moonsliver glowers but remains otherwise transfixed.

"I knew it was you all along," Snelling says.

"And yet you did nothing to stop me," Moonsliver sneers.

"I stopped you once. Even then I knew it was just a matter of time before you'd return."

I glance at Snelling, then exchange a meaningful look

with my friends. The statue was placed there on purpose. There had been an earlier breach by the Moonslivers, just like we thought.

"This time you let me run free. It's like you set out a welcome mat. It's like you wanted me here."

"I wanted no such thing," Snelling snaps, his voice so fierce the air seems to rush and hum around him.

"You did nothing to stop it."

"The choice wasn't mine to make."

Both men grow quiet, but neither backs down.

"Can someone tell me what the heck is going on here?" Boris looks from one to the other.

"It's time to end this," Snelling says. "Once and for all. And what better place than the place where it started?"

"Summerfield Lawn?" My jaw drops.

If I sound perplexed, it's because I am. Before Summerfield Lawn became a pet memorial, it was just an unused piece of land, an open field, a meadow. I never realized it had any significance in the history of Quiver Hollows.

"It's time you know the truth, Grimsly." Snelling turns to face me, and in that moment, he seems so weary that I'm overcome with worry.

Has the loss of magic, coupled with the time in the box, weakened him?

And if so—to what extent?

"There was a curse," he begins, but I'm quick to cut in.

"I know about the curse."

Snelling's brow quirks ever so slightly, but he continues. "Then you'll also know that Vitaly Moonsliver—not this Vitaly, but rather his father—"

"So you're Boris's grandfather?"

Vitaly makes a face.

Boris rolls his eyes. "Duh."

But having found one more piece of the puzzle, I just shrug.

"Boris's great-grandfather squared off with your great-grandfather." Snelling turns and pulls Ollie forward as the two descendants of former enemies turned friends turned enemies again warily eyeball each other. "To be fair, Vitaly was mired in grief. He blamed Quiver Hollows . . ." In a quieter voice, Snelling adds, "And he blamed me."

"You? Why you?" Ming asks.

But I already know the answer. Before Snelling can even get to it, I know exactly what he's going to say.

The Seer showed me.

The scene of Snelling standing in the middle of a meadow, his face bereaved, his hands dripping with blood . . .

"You're the one who delivered the baby!" I speak the long-buried truth.

Snelling's gaze saddens as Vitaly shakes with the rage of generations now gone.

"A healthy and beautiful boy," Snelling says. "Though the mother didn't live long enough to meet him."

"And we've been cursed ever since!" Moonsliver shouts. "This place will pay for what it's done to our family. And in case you doubt it, look around. Your magic is gone! And now you're exposed as the useless, incompetent fraud you always were!"

"I did everything I could." Snelling remains undeterred. "But while there was no way to save her, the child lived a long and healthy life."

Vitaly and Boris fall quiet. Here's the part they never knew, and I'm not sure I want them to know. I'm not sure I want anyone to know. And I'm pretty sure I never wanted to know. But Snelling is on a roll.

"And when that child married and had a child of his own, the curse befell him too."

"What are you getting at?" Moonsliver demands.

"All these generations of Moonslivers, both here and in the outside world, have fallen to the same sad fate. And now there are only three Moonslivers left."

"Three?" Boris looks at Vitaly, but Vitaly is no longer looking at Boris. He's looking at me. Everyone is.

I swallow and duck my head. You'd think I'd handle this better, considering I'm one of the few people here who isn't shocked by the news.

"It's you!" Moonsliver takes a step toward me. I can feel Snelling tense, ready to leap to my defense if necessary. "It is you—isn't it?"

I force my gaze to meet his. It's the best I can do.

"Of course!" Moonsliver slaps his thigh. "I should've known all along! I knew you were from here. I knew you watched over the graveyard. But I didn't realize you were one of us!"

"I'm not."

Moonsliver cocks his head to the side and studies me with fresh eyes.

"I'm not one of you. I'm nothing like you," I say, my voice firm, eyes blazing with the truth.

"You're a Moonsliver." He shrugs. "You're not actually trying to deny it now, are you?"

"I'm a Summerfield," I say with conviction. It's everything I know to be true.

"But there's no such thing." Vitaly delights. Then, looking at Snelling, he says, "Tell him the rest of the story. Tell him how he got his name."

I face Snelling, and at that moment, despite all I've been through, it feels like one of the hardest things I'll ever be called to do—to face the full truth of myself.

"This field, where you stand now," Snelling begins, "it's called Summerfield Lawn because it was once considered one of the most beautiful spots in all of Quiver Hollows. It was the one single place where the sun used to shine."

I stare at him wordlessly. I couldn't speak if I wanted to. My tongue feels immobile, my lips parched and dry. This is the lawn I saw in the hologram, only I didn't recognize it then.

"It's the place where Vitaly met his wife, Maris. It's also the place where Vitaly was ejected right out of our world."

Beside me, my friends gasp.

"But while Vitaly vanished, the baby remained. And those of us present decided to give the child a new name." Snelling turns to me then. "We named him Grimsly Summerfield. That child, born a Moonsliver, was your great-great-grandfather."

Boris looks me over and scowls. Vitaly shakes his head and says, "Guess that proves it. Like it or not, you're one of us, kid. Which means you bear the curse too." And for some reason he laughs, although I fail to find a single word of it funny.

"Technically speaking, I am a Moonsliver," I grudgingly admit. "But the connection stops there. Snelling raised me. It's his values I share, not yours. You're both hateful, cynical, power-hungry control freaks. You're ruled by your egos and fueled by revenge. But what you don't understand is that underneath all the bullying and name-calling and pushing people around, you're both cowards. It's easy to be negative and skeptical of everything you see. It ensures you never have to risk anything—like looking foolish or having your heart crushed by grief. But it takes courage and bravery to allow yourself to be open to the possibility of miracles, to find magical moments where and when you least expect them. It takes faith to see the goodness in people who, on the outside, anyway, appear to be nothing like you."

By the time I finish, I'm out of breath, but Boris just rolls his eyes and shakes his head. "Whatever, Gutter Rat!" He folds his arms across his chest. "You're right—you're not a Moonsliver. Clearly you're too big of a loser to be one of us."

"Man, you just never learn, do you?"

The voice makes me pause. It's the last one I expected to hear, but one I definitely recognize. I can't stop the grin that creeps across my face when I turn to find Frankie, flanked by Wolfhart and Fogbottom.

FORTY-SEVEN

SPELL SPINNER

"Even your girlfriend the Spell Spinner can't save your town now," Boris says.

"She's not my girlfriend." I'm quick to correct him.

My words overlap with Frankie's as she shakes her head and says, "Boris, you seriously need to get over yourself. And, Headmaster Moonsliver"—she looks him dead in the eye—"bad news for you: your academy is under investigation and is in the process of being shut down." Then she turns to me. "Turns out a lot of those orphans weren't actually orphans. Some were missing children." She wags a finger at Vitaly.

"You've done very bad things, and now you have nowhere to go. Though I hear there's a vacancy in the hole."

Moonsliver scoffs. "You don't know anything. That was always your problem—you always thought you were so much smarter than you are."

I glance at Frankie, ready to jump in and help, but she doesn't need me to come to her rescue. She's got this all on her own.

"And you two." Moonsliver gestures toward Wolfhart and Fogbottom. "I think you're both smart enough to know which side you should be on."

I watch as they exchange an uncertain look.

"Don't listen to their nonsense. This place belongs to us now. Did you see our statue in the town square? Did you see the sign right beside it? Quiver Hollows is no more. It's Moonsliver Landing now. And once we rid the place of freaks, we have big plans for developing the town. There will be hotels, casinos, office towers, shopping malls, apartment buildings, maybe even that amusement park Vitaly always dreamed of. Sky's the limit, anything's possible! And if you play your cards right, you can both be … well, not exactly in charge; those positions are reserved for Boris and I, obviously, but you can certainly be in top management for sure. What do you say? More than these rejects can offer."

He glances between them as Frankie says, "Boris and me."

"What?" Moonsliver squints.

"You said 'Boris and I,' when it's really 'Boris and me.' Obviously."

His face darkens.

"I mean, honestly. What kind of headmaster are you?"

"The kind you should fear. And let me be clear: like the rest of these freaks, there's no place for you either."

"Boris, Wolfhart, Fogbottom!" He turns away, fully expecting them to follow, when Frankie retrieves the enchanted scroll from her waistband and begins to read from it.

"What're you doing?" I peer over her shoulder, trying to see what she sees, but to me it just looks like a bunch of symbols and images floating across an old yellowing piece of parchment.

Frankie's voice thunders, growing stronger, deeper with each spoken word. And though Moonsliver tries to retreat, it's as though he's trying to outrun a force stronger than him. He's rooted in place.

I glance at Snelling trying to catch a glimpse of insight into what might be happening, but his gaze remains fixed on Frankie, who continues the chant.

Ming hovers nervously. Ollie stares, transfixed. Wolfhart and Fogbottom freeze, not knowing what to expect.

Deep within the soil, the earth begins to tremble, the scorched lawn beneath my feet quivering and shaking. Frankie's incantation grows stronger, more insistent, as portions of the ground begin to give way.

A long, pointy root reaches up from the depths, snares Vitaly by the ankles, and slowly starts dragging him down.

Boris screams and tries to escape, but it's only a moment later when more roots pop up and latch on to him.

"Make it stop!" Boris shrieks, looking to Vitaly to do something.

But Vitaly is too busy losing the battle against the long-armed roots yanking him deeper and deeper into the earth.

"I command you to stop!" Vitaly screams. "I command you to stop before this goes any further!"

"She's merely granting the wish that's guided you for all these years," Snelling murmurs.

Vitaly looks frantic, Boris is crying, and from out of the deepest layers of soil new roots are unearthed, these covered in maggots and worms.

"She's reversing the curse," Snelling tells them.

Frankie reads without faltering, continuing the recitation.

"What about him?" Vitaly cries. He's buried up to his shoulders now, but he struggles to yank an arm free so he can point a finger at me. "He's a Moonsliver! Why isn't it taking him too?"

"I already told you," I said. "I'm a Summerfield, which means I'm nothing like you."

The earth continues to tremble and shake as more roots, more worms, more creatures rise and clutch Boris and Vitaly. Curling around them, slithering into their nostrils, clasping their necks until their faces turn purple. They drag them deeper and deeper, until their screams are completely smothered and we can no longer see them.

When it's over, when the earth finally stills and the Moonslivers are gone, Frankie lets out a deeply satisfied sigh.

Then she carefully tucks the scroll back into her waistband and introduces herself to Snelling and my friends.

"I'm Frankie Husker," she says. "But you can call me the Spell Spinner."

FORTY-EIGHT

DEARLY BELOVED

"Are they really gone?" Wolfhart peers at the dirt as though trying to detect some last trace of them. The earth has settled in a way that makes it seem as though nothing even happened.

"They're gone," Snelling assures him. "For good this time."

"What now?" Ollie asks.

It's the same question I've been thinking. That, along with: What's become of Penelope?

And: How did Frankie and Wolfhart and Fogbottom get here when there's a wall surrounding the property?

As though reading my mind, Frankie says, "We took the tunnel. A different tunnel. They must've been working on it for years."

"We'll have to close it up," I say. "We'll have to get on that right away—"

"No." Snelling runs a hand through his beard, looking wizened and weary. "No more walls. No more hiding from the outside world."

"But I'm not sure the world is ready for this place," Wolfhart says, then quickly adds, "No offense."

"And none taken," Snelling says. "Don't get me wrong—the dome of fog, clouds, and mist will always be there." He cranes his neck to look overhead; then, seeing how much it's diminished, he adds, "Well, some semblance of it, anyway. But when Yegor Quiver first came here, there were no walls, no overt attempts to keep people out. The only thing that kept people away was their own unwillingness to believe that something better existed outside of what they were taught. And if Yegor hadn't found his way here, well, we wouldn't have the School for Spoon Bending, the Manifesters Academy, the fourth-grade tightrope-walking challenge. Heck, we wouldn't have Ollie." He ruffles Ollie's hair. "And we certainly wouldn't have Grimsly and his wonderful pet funerals." Snelling shoots me a tired grin. "We wouldn't have any of those delightful things."

"But we also wouldn't have had the Moonslivers and all

the trouble they've caused." I study the spot where I watched them get sucked into the earth, bothered by the idea of them somehow resurfacing.

"But aren't you worried?" Ming says. "About what their hateful DNA might do to our land once it all mixes in?"

"They're a permanent part of our story," Snelling says. "They always were. And there's always a great deal of value to be found in the contrasts. If not for the dark, you wouldn't recognize the light. If not for hate, you wouldn't know love. If not for evil, you'd fail to recognize goodness. It's the opposites of things that are most defining."

The words settle around us, and after a moment, Fogbottom clears his throat and says, "We saved two barrels. Just like you asked. Maybe we should start spreading it around and return it to the land?"

I stay behind with Snelling, watching as my friends pull the two remaining barrels from the bed of the truck. "It's the bones from the graves," I explain. Then I go on to tell him everything that happened since I last saw him, or I give him the condensed version, anyway.

"I met the Seer." I study his face, looking for some sort of giveaway, but Snelling maintains an inscrutable expression. "She told me she knew you."

"Did she?" His eyes spark just a bit, but the flame fades so quickly I'm left wondering if maybe I imagined it.

I consider confiding all the rest, telling him about one of the Seer's biggest regrets, but then I figure he probably already knows. And if not, well, it's probably not the best time to reveal the love story that could've been but never was. To be honest, Snelling isn't looking so good.

"You okay, sir?" I ask.

Snelling lowers his chin and considers me for a long, sobering moment. And when he finally talks, it's as though the words are being spoken from a faraway place. "Long ago, I too asked the Seer for a glimpse of my future. . . ."

My belly churns as I wait for him to continue.

"Grimsly, I've lived an awfully long life, a very good and fulfilled life, and now—"

"No!" Suddenly, my head is swimming and my eyes are bleary, but I'm committed to doing whatever it takes to stop him from saying what he's determined to say. "No!" I repeat. "This can't happen. I'm not ready!"

"You may not feel ready, but look at all you've accomplished! Look at all you've done! Grimsly, I'm so proud of you. Ever since I discovered you in Summerfield Lawn, surrounded by a fluffle of bunnies, I knew you'd come to replace me as the Keeper."

"You were the Keeper?" I blurt. The shock of his statement renders me temporarily oblivious to everything else. My mind reels backward, searching for hints, clues, hidden signs I might've missed. Though I guess it only makes sense there was a Keeper before me and that it just so happened to be Snelling.

"I was," he admits, his breath growing increasingly heavy and labored. "I also knew this day would come, and I never once doubted you would turn it around. My only regret is that I didn't prepare you. I delayed the conversation until it was already too late."

"Wolfhart!" I shout, my voice drowning out Snelling's words. I don't want his praise. I don't want his remorse. I want him to live!

"Do you know why you were able to bend that metal and save us?"

I shake my head. I don't care. None of it matters. He's here. I saved them. Onward and upward!

"Because you weren't trying to impress me, or prove something to yourself . . ."

"Fogbottom!" I scream. "Get over here—*now!*"

Snelling places his hand over mine, his long talons softly scratching my skin, his rows of rings glinting. He insists that I hear him. "The reason it worked this time is because you were working toward a greater good."

I stare at him breathless, my vision blurred with tears.

"This had nothing to do with your ego—you were driven by service—serving those you love most. I'm so very proud of you. I always knew you had it in you."

His lids begin to flutter closed, but I can't let that happen. Can't let that—

"Fogbottom, Frankie, Ming!" I scream their names at the top of my lungs. "Bring me the bone dust! Bring me—"

I haven't even finished when Snelling slumps to the ground.

FORTY-NINE

MASTERPIECE IN THE MAKING

I saw this part too.

I never told anyone. I didn't want to admit it to myself or chance spending too much time thinking about it.

I refused to give it any more power than it deserved and risk increasing the odds of it becoming real.

Though I did ask the Seer about it.

One of the last things I asked, just before I left, was if Snelling would be okay.

And while she avoided claiming he would, she also declined to say that he wouldn't.

She told me the future was malleable, flexible, and mine to determine.

Well, all I know for sure is that I'm not ready to lose Snelling. Not even close.

He has so much left to teach me.

I have so much more to learn.

I hover over him, desperately seeking a pulse, a faint breath—any sign of life will do. But I'm so overcome by panic I can't get a read.

"Ming!" I cry. "Hurry!"

In an instant Ming lands beside me, her palms filled with bone dust that she carefully funnels between Snelling's lips.

"He lost all his magic," she says. "When we were inside that box, I could tell he was faltering. The only reason he hung on for so long is because he wanted to witness you bending that metal."

I struggle to see through my grief.

"We were the doubters." She lowers her gaze in shame. "But Snelling was sure you'd succeed." After a moment she adds, "Maybe we need more?" She nods at Snelling, who shows no sign of recovery.

"Maybe," I say, unsure of anything anymore. I just hold Snelling's head in my lap and repeat the Seer's words in my head.

The future is malleable, flexible, and mine to determine.

Thefutureismalleableflexibleandminetodeterminethefuture ismalleableflexibleandminetodeterminethefutu—

"He okay?" Ollie slides in beside us and offers more bone dust.

I feed it to Snelling, but it's impossible to tell if it's having any effect.

reismalleableflexibleandminetodeterminethefutureismalleable flexibleandminetodeterminethefutureis—

"What now?" Fogbottom says.

Frankie looks around, surveying the grounds. "We wait, I guess."

malleableflexibleandminetodeterminethefutureismalleable flexibleandminetodeterminethefutureis—

From seemingly out of nowhere, Penelope appears, a vision of pale skin, elfin ears, mismatched eyes, and flaming-red hair, a fluffle of healthy, happy bunnies surrounding her feet.

"You made it!" Ming leaps up to hug her as Ollie does the same, but I remain beside Snelling, repeating my new mantra in my head.

malleableflexibleandminetodeterminethefutureismalleable flexibleandminetodeterminethefutureis—

After Ollie and Ming introduce her and catch her up on everything that's happening, Penelope comes to sit beside me.

"You're right," she thinks. *"The future really is malleable, flexible, and ours to determine."*

I look at her. Normally I wouldn't like that she's reading

my mind, but nothing about this moment is normal. Including the fact that I can now hear what she's thinking.

"So what do you say we paint a picture of the future together?"

She gestures for me to lift both my hands: then she places her palms flush against mine.

"Always begin with a clean canvas," she instructs. *"And when you're ready, feel free to make the first brushstroke."*

"I've never done this before, I—"

"Fine, then I'll start. But you go next. After all, this will determine the kind of world we'll be living in."

I close my eyes, and in my mind, I watch Penelope fill in the edges and corners of the canvas by painting a lush turquoise-tinged lawn shaded by vibrant trees with flowering vines looped and curled around long, knotty limbs. There's not a single wall in sight.

When it's my turn, I add to the landscape by restoring the pet memorials, returning the stream to its former lovely shade of rainbow, warping the trees in the forest, and making Pendulum Falls act like a water zipper once more—flowing down and up and back down again.

In the town's square I return the statue of Yegor Quiver to its rightful place. Then I go about repairing all the shops by fixing the broken windows, ripping the boards off the doors, and scrubbing the graffiti from the walls.

And just when I think I'm done, Penelope prompts, *"Aren't you forgetting something?"*

I grin as I begin adding in all the animals and people. The colorful bunnies and the dogs that give birth to purple piglets, along with the girls with scales, the boys with tails, and Albie with his bulging fish eyes. I mend Ming's dress, making the feathers bounce and flutter again. And I change Frankie and Wolfhart and Fogbottom out of the stiff, boring uniforms they were forced to wear and into clothes that are much better suited to them.

For a moment, I consider changing the Seer, wondering if it's possible to undo the choice she made.

But then I decide against it, and I paint her crazy see-sawing house at the top of the mountain. I even keep the flesh-eating vines, the spiked stairway, and the gate Snelling made.

Inside that house I create a lazy, oversized cat. And his mysterious owner, permanently stuck at age nine.

I have no right to determine her future—that's for her to decide.

"And you?" Penelope nudges.

I think hard on this one. Do I want to return to the Grimsly Summerfield I was?

Or do I want to become someone completely different than I ever imagined I could be?

While I can never go back to the person I was at the start of this journey, that doesn't mean I have to abandon him completely. So I include a picture of myself in my black suit and white shirt with my messenger bag strapped across my chest and my hair returned to its usual mop of long bangs. After all, I'm the Keeper. I have a pet graveyard named after me. Keeping the bones safe is a big responsibility. And I don't plan on leaving it unprotected anytime soon.

But not wanting to forget where I've been, I paint on a navy blue cap with the letters *N* and *Y* intersecting each other.

And next to me, I paint Snelling. With his long braid, his curlicue mustache, and blue beard, he wraps an arm around me and I know without question that I've always belonged here.

"And me?" Penelope inquires.

I hand over the brush. "That's for you to determine."

A small grin lights up Penelope's face as she paints an exact replica of herself as she is right now.

"What can I say?" She laughs. *"I like being me. Anything else?"*

I take a moment to consider. Then I dot the canvas with white and silver in an effort to restore the perpetual dome of fog, clouds, and mist that surrounds us. Not to keep people out, but because I like seeing it that way. Also, I've come to realize the integral role it plays in keeping the flowers in bloom, the grass vibrant and turquoise. But right over Summerfield Lawn I leave the top open.

According to Snelling, it was once the loveliest spot in all of Quiver Hollows, a place where the sun used to shine. And if you can see the sun, then that means at night you can see the moon and stars too. From now on, I promise myself I'll take the time to appreciate that view.

When we agree that we're finished, we open our eyes to watch the earth churning around us, healing itself with new turquoise-tinged blades. The trees stretch and yawn as though waking from a deep slumber, their branches reaching low, smoothing away all the dead and blackened bark and making way for the new. Flowering vines loop and curl, the pet memorials stand tall once again, and Quiver Hollows breathes with new life, looking just like the painting Penelope and I created.

Beside me, Snelling rises and stirs and looks around.

"What's happening?" he asks, his face illuminated by the glow of the sun shining overhead.

"Quiver Hollows is weird again," I say. "That's what's happening."

He tweaks the brim of my hat and slides an arm around me, and with Ollie, Ming, Penelope, Frankie, Wolfhart, and Fogbottom gathered around us, we watch our world return to life.

ACKNOWLEDGMENTS

Writing is usually a solitary endeavor, but I was lucky enough to work on this book at a lovely writing retreat surrounded by good friends. Special thanks to the Swan Valley crew: Wendy Toliver, Emily Wing Smith, Allison van Diepen, Linda Gerber, Kristin Harmel, and Jay Asher for the endless laughs and late-night chats.

A huge bundle of gratitude to everyone at Delacorte, with a special shout-out to my wonderful editor, Krista Vitola, for being insightful, kind, and an absolute pleasure to work with.

Also, many thanks to my agent, Bill Contardi—I'm so grateful to have you on my team.

And, as always, much thanks to Sandy for absolutely everything.

ABOUT THE AUTHOR

Alyson Noël is the award-winning number one *New York Times* bestselling author of twenty-three novels, including the series the Immortals, Riley Bloom, and the Soul Seekers. Born and raised in Orange County, California, she has lived in both Mykonos and Manhattan and is now settled back in Southern California. Visit her at alysonnoel.com, and follow her on Facebook and Twitter.